LITTLE BLACK BOOK
EVILyn Reigns

Little Black Book

Copyright 2023 © EVILyn Reigns

The unauthorized reproduction or distribution of this copyrighted work is a crime punishable by law. No part of this book may be scanned, uploaded to, or downloaded from file sharing sites or distributed in any other way via the internet or any other means, electronic or print, without the publisher's permission. Criminal copyright infringement, including infringement without monetary gain, is investigated by the FBI and is punishable by up to 5 years in federal prison and a fine of $250,000.

All rights reserved. Except as permitted under the U.S. Copyright Act of 1976.No part of this publication may be reproduced, stored in, or introduced into a retrieval system or transmitted, in any form or by any means (electronic, mechanical, photocopying, recording, or otherwise), without the prior permission of EVILyn Reigns.

Editing and Formatting: Beth A. Freely
Cover Design: Dark Water Covers

Dedication

When I began this story, this was just another horror/thriller that I had brewing in my head. As I began to invest in the story, my best friend's cancer progressed past the point of treatment. I took several days off from work and stayed with her, helping my friend, my soulmate, as she battled the debilitating disease that had her wasting away before my eyes. The demons took over my mind as I worked at her bedside, listening to her struggling to breathe. At one point she woke up and smiled at me and told me that the click clack of my computer was so very soothing to her because she knew I was next to her bedside.

I feel as if all the negative emotions from the most traumatizing experience of my life went into this book.

Every. Single. Emotion.

She passed away on February 28, 2023.

This book goes out to my very best friend, my soulmate. I wouldn't be where I am today if it wasn't for her. She shaped my life for the better during the twenty years that we've been together, and I will be forever grateful to have known her.

This book also goes out to all who have lost someone to cancer or who may be battling this disease. I pray that you will survive and murder the cancer that is trying to snuff out your own life. Fight! Don't give up. And when you are ready to take your last breath, just remember that you are loved, you are remembered, and you will remain immortal in the stories that your friends and family share with the world.

Be aware that when you open this book, every time a person dies between these pages, I am trying to kill cancer.

Because cancer sucks!

WARNING!

This book contains situations that contain trauma inducing scenes. *Little Black Book* is a BDSM fiction story that is filled with scenes of sexual assault, rape, violence, and strong language.

Other Books by EVILyn Reigns

Abnormal Carnage

Chapter 1

The quiet tomb of the public library after hours had two different feelings. The first feeling was a haunted essence of stories from the past, millions of lore that filled the cardboard and leatherette bindings. Add to it the smell at the end of the evening and it could overwhelm an ordinary person's most insensitive of senses. But to a woman that had extraordinary perceptions of the world around her, the scent could render her senseless.

EVILyn Reigns

The monotone beeping of the scanner rendered Kat mindless. The constant beep of the wand as it hovered over barcodes was the background noise to a mindless task, one that she almost welcomed at the end of a long evening. Droves of people visited the library daily, ranging from the elderly looking for companionship to the college students cramming for tests.

There was also the rare middle-aged man who would try to win a date from her by trying to charm her. Unfortunately for them, she was unable to be charmed. That feeling was forever taken away from her as a young child and she knew that it would never return.

The second feeling was euphoria. Late in the evening when the library was finally closed and she felt at peace, escaping the lingering memories that recurred daily and plagued her each minute of every day with any person that tried to engage with her. The peace and quiet of the closed library gave her harmony from the barrage of people's thoughts. Oh, she couldn't read thoughts. That was a fake psychic magician's trick. But Kat could read faces and body language and she knew the gross inhuman thoughts of the male and female population. It took every bone in her body to keep her inner demons from reacting.

Kat stacked the last of the books on the rolling cart for the morning shift and stood up from her chair, stretching her arms over her head. She groaned as her back muscles popped. Leaning down, she placed her favorite purple high heeled stilettoes back onto her sore feet and grabbed her bag. For a librarian that was on her feet all day, her shoes weren't exactly the best, but she had a slight addiction to height. Standing at only five feet, Kat was one of the shortest people in the library. She noticed that having that extra four inches of height also gave her a modicum of respect that she felt she lacked with her shorter stature.

Passing the mirror near the front door, Kat stopped to look at her reflection. The nightly ritual before leaving the library had her removing the pin from her bun and finger brushing the long red curls that flowed down her back. Her temples always began to hurt towards the end of her shift because of the tightness of her bun and the release of her hair, the dissipation of the pain on her scalp, was almost orgasmic. Kat slowly traced the old scars down her face, a reminder of her childhood that followed her with every glance into the mirror. She stopped using makeup to cover the white lines years ago and decided to embrace the physical flaws that were forced upon her a lifetime ago. The years had passed but the memories of her trauma still felt as fresh as if it happened yesterday.

    Shaking her head, Kat walked out of the large library, her heels clicking with every step on the shiny marble floor. Opening the main door, the hot San Antonio air hit her face. Sweat bubbled on her forehead as she locked the door and began to walk toward her car parked in a lot on the side of the building. Kat's hair already felt heavy with the humidity that hung in the summer air. She smiled when she spied her car, her most prized possession. It was her first purchase after she escaped from her home, the first happy memory since her

Little Black Book

emancipation from the horrors of that place. The older sedan, a Buick LeSabre, was a boring tan color, the inside just as boring as the outside, but sitting in her car and breathing in the scent of the soft leather gave her inner demons some level of peace. Unfortunately, not enough peace. Not tonight.

Kat drove toward her home, aching for a long bath, a tall glass of wine, and the low drone of the television that would chase away the aching, silent loneliness of her apartment. She didn't keep any memories in her home. There weren't any framed pictures of her family hanging on her walls. Her apartment was almost sterile with the lack of living that she had left behind. No, the only prized possession was her car.

Opening the front door of her apartment, Kat set her purse on the table in the foyer and locked the deadbolt behind her. She stripped her shoes from her aching feet and wiggled her toes against the soft carpet. She stretched her aching arms over her head and headed to her bedroom, stripping her pencil skirt from her hips, and throwing it into the laundry basket

EVILyn Reigns

in the corner of her room. Throwing herself onto her bed, she moaned as she wiggled into the mattress. For a few minutes, she laid in her bed, clad in only her button-down shirt and thong, wishing for sleep to overtake her but knowing that her nightmares would prevent her from having a decent night sleep.

She huffed in frustration and began to unbutton her shirt, leaving it open as she stood up from her bed. Her stomach was crying out for some dinner and her body was demanding a hot bath to soak in. As Kat walked into the kitchen, a knocking on her door had her changing direction and she looked through the peep hole of her front door. She smiled as she opened it.

"Is that the way you welcome all your guests, my lady?"

Kat giggled and ushered one of her best friends into her apartment. The smells wafting from the bag he carried relieved her. She hated cooking for herself, and it smelled like her favorite Chinese dish.

"What did you bring me?" Kat asked as she followed Josh into the kitchen. At five-foot-six-inches and 120 pounds, Josh was slim, skinny even, but he could eat like a football linebacker. She would have normally covered up with a robe with any other man that may have visited, but her best friend wasn't into women. He liked the male population more than she did.

"I brought you Kung Pow Chicken and spring rolls. Your favorite. I'm starting to think that the only reason you order the Kung Pow chicken every time we have Chinese is because you know that I can't stand it. Ugh, the smell alone has me wanting to yak."

"Well, if you would quit eating my food, I wouldn't have to stoop so low."

Kat sat at the kitchen table, pulling her feet up under her bottom, and reached for the takeout container her friend offered her.

"Seriously, you're not going to even get dressed?" Josh asked as he sat across the table from her.

EVILyn Reigns

She stared into his brown eyes as the corners of his eyes crinkled with humor. She loved his humor and the way he teased her.

"Well, if you were attracted to me at all, I maybe would have covered up. But I don't have to worry about you fantasizing about my body."

"I'm not gay at all. No ma'am. I'm faking it actually. Totally faking it. I'm getting hard now staring at your perfect breasts."

Kat threw a fortune cookie at her friend, giggling. "I'm not falling for that. I walked in on you with that Scott guy a few weeks ago. My pure virginal eyes will never recover. I still have nightmares after that incident. Especially after I saw the size of that monster. Tell me, how on earth did he get it to fit?"

Josh threw the fortune cookie back at her. "Shush… it's all a ploy to get into your pants. I first come in as your gay best friend, gain your trust, then I impress you with my manly prowess. How am I doing so far? Are you ready to jump my bones?"

Little Black Book

Holding a napkin over her mouth as she laughed, Kat swallowed before answering. "Not so much, no. But if your buddy, Scott, ever decides to straighten his ruler, tell him to call me." She made a telephone gesture with her hand and held it to her ear, giggling when Josh thew another fortune cookie at her.

"Well, I didn't come over here just to feed you, love. I have ulterior motives. Finish your meal, get dressed and come out with me tonight. It's Friday night; we need to go out. Also, Jenna asked us to stop by the club and pick her up."

Kat nodded and took another bite of her meal. Jenna was her other best friend. The three of them had been friends since they were 18. She was surprised that the three of them had been together for the last ten years. Jenna was an extremely beautiful woman and her and Josh had to protect her from a lot of creeps over the years. Her dark skin and gypsy eyes drew everyone's attention, attention that Kat hated but dealt with because Jenna couldn't help it.

EVILyn Reigns

"I'm going to go change," Kat said as she stood up from the table and placed her leftovers in the refrigerator. She walked back to her room and removed her dress shirt, throwing it in the same basket as the skirt. Opening her closet, she began to look through her clothing, unsatisfied with all of her outfits.

"Do you need some help, *Meuf*?" Josh asked from the doorway. She smiled at his French slang and nodded. She remembered him trying to take a French class back in college and failing when all he would remember was slang and curse words.

"I'm not sure where we're going. I'm kind of in a dark mood so I'm not feeling any of my skirts. Where are you taking us?"

Shuffling through her closet, Josh hmphed and pulled out a leather vest that was hiding in the back. "We're going to S & P, and if you're feeling dark, you should dress the part. No arguments. Wear the vest and the leather pants. Maybe you might get lucky with some poor unsuspecting soul later

Little Black Book

tonight." Josh began to hum the song from *Little Mermaid* as she slipped the vest on over her bra.

"Nuh-uh. Remove the bra. Let the girls fly. Freedom!" he yelled as he walked out of her room.

Kat giggled and took off her bra and put the vest back on. Josh seemed to be in a mood as well. Tonight might be fun.

EVILyn Reigns

Chapter 2

Kat and Josh walked into the gentleman's club, Garnet Embrace. They walked over to the bar and sat down, both of them looking around for Jenna. Their friend was a part time cocktail waitress and part time bartender. She used to be a teacher but quit after only a year when she found she could make more money and perform less work waitressing. Kat swore up and down that Jenna secretly stripped on the side. There was no other way that girl could afford her lavish lifestyle as a waitress.

EVILyn Reigns

"Where is she?" Josh asked, looking around.

"I don't know. Let me ask the bartender." Kat waved the bartender over and the woman glowered at the two of them.

"Is Jenna off her shift yet?" Kat asked.

"You have to buy a drink if you want to wait at the bar," the other woman sneered. Kat rolled her eyes and removed a twenty from her front vest pocket.

"One shot of tequila for me and a Bloody Mary for princess over here," Kat said as she motioned toward Josh with her head.

"As if. I heard that, hussy."

The bartender quickly handed Kat her shot and started working on the Bloody Mary as a shadow fell over her. She looked up and smiled as Jenna sat at the bar next to her. Her short brown curls were falling out of her ponytail and her dark skin glistened with sweat from a long shift. She wore the club uniform shirt, twisted high and knotted under her breasts, exposing her tight stomach.

Little Black Book

"Whatcha drinking?" Jenna asked, her brown eyes sparkling with humor.

"Tea," Kat said as she took a sip.

Jenna reached over and snagged the shot glass from Kat. She took a whiff and wrinkled her nose at the bitter smell. "This doesn't smell like any kind of tea I've seen."

"Okay, tea-quila."

Jenna threw her head back and laughed as the bartender handed Josh his drink. He saluted Jenna with his glass and said, "Tomato juice."

The three of them laughed and Kat downed the rest of her shot. "You about done here? Josh said that we're headed to the S & P."

The S & P was their favorite weekend haunt. The club was a secret BDSM organization that catered to the many proclivities found in the city of San Antonio. Nobody knew what the 'S' and 'P' stood for so the three of them used to come up with different nicknames until one day Josh said Strokers & Pokers. After that name, the game was over, and the S & P would forever be named Strokers &Pokers.

EVILyn Reigns

Too bad the manager didn't feel the same way about the new name that Josh created. They sent in multiple correspondence suggesting the new name but it still remained S & P.

"I don't think Josh is done with his 'tomato juice' quite yet," Jenna said. "Let me go change my clothes and then we'll head out. Kat, how are you feeling tonight?"

Kat licked the rim of her shot glass and glowered at her friend. "I'm in a mood."

Jenna shivered and smiled before walking away. Kat figured that she was anticipating what the night might bring. She pointed to her drink and handed the bartender another ten, sipping at the new drink that was placed down in front of her. Another woman sat in the stool next to Kat and reached over to finger comb Kat's hair. Kat grabbed the woman's hand.

"Sapphire, I'm not in the mood. Go away." The woman huffed, flipped her long blonde hair over her shoulder and walked away, sashaying her hips. All of the strippers in the club had gemstone stage names and they all tried to get Kat alone. They had no clue what Kat needed, and she knew that the women would run screaming if they ever found out.

"How is it you get all the sexy men and women? It's really not fair," Josh lamented as he licked a little drop of the drink from his lips.

"I don't get all of them. I am still waiting for Scott's deets. Then I will finally have world domination by seducing the entire gay community."

Kat smiled as he laughed out loud, and they both stood up as Jenna joined them. "Okay, who's driving?" she asked. The shiny silver tunic hugged Jenna's curves and her black jeans were so tight, Kat wondered how the girl even buttoned them.

Kat looked over at Josh. "Speed Racer got his license suspended again so it's up to me to be the chauffeur… again. I swear, between the two of you, I need to start charging Uber fees."

"I wasn't going that fast. The cop caught me didn't he?"

Jenna laughed as they followed Kat out of the gentleman's club and to the car parked in the lot.

EVILyn Reigns

Jenna climbed into the backseat as Josh sat in the front. Kat looked into the rearview mirror at her friend.

"Are we going to Strokers for any particular reason, Jen?"

Kat watched her friend shiver and shake her head. "Like you, I'm in a mood and I need to recharge. You won't leave me, right?"

"Never. I would never leave you. It's the pact that I'll never break. We won't let you ever get hurt and you both stop me from hurting others." Kat reached into the backseat and the two women clasped hands.

"Don't forget me, you hookers. I swear I'm the lone guy out in this group." The three of them held hands for a moment and then Kat broke contact and started the car, driving into the night.

Chapter 3

Music drummed along with her heartbeat as it beat hard in her chest. Kat and Jenna held hands as they walked through the club, strobe lights flickering into the dark bar. Bodies crushed against one another on the dance floor as the overwhelming smell of alcohol and sweat assaulted Kat's senses. She pushed a man from her that tried to drag her onto the dance floor and was stopped in the rising momentum of violence by Jenna's hand on her arm. The three of them finally arrived at the back door, barred and guarded by a burly security bouncer, quintessential humongous arms crossed over his robust chest.

"Jeebs, allow us entry, man," Joshua said as he tipped his imaginary hat, his blonde hair with its blue tips covering his eyes. Kat shook her head and pulled her black key card from the front pocket of her vest, swiping it over the keyless lock. The door clicked and the guard stepped aside as the trio walked through, the heavy bass and cloying smells of the club silenced by the closing of the iron door. Kat walked over to the front desk and used her keycard again at the computer, signing the three of them in.

The S & P was a long-time secret club for the BDSM crowd. The three of them had been members for the last few years, ever since they discovered each other's kinks and helped each other develop their sexuality, safely. Jenna seemed to have the worst one. She needed to feel pain, to be hurt during sex, in order to orgasm. Jenna was always worried about searching out someone to help her with her sexual kink ever since she was severely hurt by her ex-boyfriend a year ago. After Kat found her bloodied and bruised in Jenna's home, they vowed to never let her search for her high alone. Kat knew it was a high because she herself searched for her own extreme soar. Kat's tastes ran along the way of inflicting pain. When Jenna became too restless, Kat would help her friend in the only way she knew how.

The woman at the front desk clicked a few keys. "You will be in room six. Would you like your usual?"

Kat nodded and took the key from the receptionist. The two women walked back to their rented room. She looked behind her to see Josh checking in as well. He was a bit of a wild card. He kind of liked it all. Josh knew how to use the leather and how to take the leather and she wasn't sure which he preferred just yet.

Kat ushered Jenna into the room and closed the door behind her. Jenna kneeled on the divan, her back to Kat. "How much do you need, Jenna?"

"I need it hard," she answered.

EVILyn Reigns

Kat removed the small crop from the wall and rubbed her hand over the leather. She then walked up to Jenna and slowly traced the crop over her neck.

"Remove all your clothes. Lay on the bed and place the restraints around your neck and wrists."

She watched as Jenna took off her shirt. She folded it neatly and laid it on the floor. She then removed her shoes, socks, and pants, folding them as well before standing completely naked. She faced Kat and sat down silently on the divan before reaching for the collar and the leather cuffs, restraining herself as she was told. Kat walked around to the back of the divan and pulled the chain, tightening Jenna's hands above her head.

"What's our codes?" Kat asked.

"Pineapple to slow down. Apple to stop."

Kat nodded and began to slowly trace the crop around Jenna's breasts, lifting one and then the other with the end of the rod. Without warning, she lashed at Jenna's breasts, leaving behind small red welts on the top of her skin. Jenna moaned as the ministration of the whip matched the drum of the muffled music that echoed in the club. Blood began to pound in Kat's head as she watched her friend writhe and groan with every lash she bestowed on Jenna's darkened skin.

"Are you ready?" Kat whispered, stepping back from her friend's now still body. The only part moving was her chest as she gulped large amounts of air. Jenna nodded and wiggled against the restraints.

"No, you need to tell me. Are you ready?"

"Yes. I'm ready. Yes," Jenna moaned, and Kat walked over to the door, unlocking it. She knocked three times. A large, older man in his 30s walked into the room, his dark hair slicked back. A beard covered his face, his eyes the only feature she looked into as she waved him toward the naked body that squirmed on the divan.

"You know the rules?" she asked their regular. He looked down into her eyes and nodded before walking over to Jenna. Kat heard the crinkling of the condom wrapper as she turned away from them. She sat on the armchair across the room from the couple and pulled a bottle of tequila from the mini fridge against the wall. She poured herself two fingers of the liquor and sipped slowly as she watched the couple fuck on the small bed, his hips pumping into her, the wet heat slapping with every thrust.

"I need more. It's not enough. Kat I need more!" Jenna screamed.

Kat sat her drink down and stood up, grasping a leather flushing whip that hung from the wall. "Turn her over," she demanded from Jenna's partner. The man twisted around and laid back on the divan, pulling Jenna on top of his hips. She cried out as the cuffs tightened around her neck and wrists. Jenna's back was to Kat, and he began to fuck her harder as she sat on him, her moans weakened with the loss of her breath.

"You good, Jen?" Her friend groaned and barely nodded. "I need the answer, Jen. Are you good?" Kat insisted.

"Yes!" Jenna yelled before Kat began to use the flushing whip on her back, multiple small red welts bubbling the skin with every strike.

Little Black Book

"Harder!" Jenna screamed to both Kat and the man that fucked her. Blood began to well up on her skin as Kat's strokes strengthened. She could feel the euphoria build up in her own core, wet heat swelling up her vaginal lips with every stroke she bestowed, and every drop of blood Kat lotted.

"Pineapple!" Jenna whispered.

Kat quickly stopped and backed away, allowing the couple to finish fucking. Grunts and slaps filled the air, the smell of sex overpowering the small room. Kat sat back on the chair, took a sip of her tequila, then reached her own hand into her tight pants to masturbate along with the fucking couple. Visions of blood, red welts, and cries from Jenna brought Kat to completion as she heard Jenna scream with her own orgasm.

EVILyn Reigns

Chapter 4

Kat stood up from her chair as their partner backed away from Jenna. He grabbed his pants from where he discarded them near the door and put them on. Kat handed him a wad of cash and opened the door, quickly shutting and locking the door behind him. S & P had some very illegal business practices, prostitution being one of them. Kat always requested the same man for their trysts, since he knew their rules and did his job, leaving without trying to upsell them. She turned back to Jenna on the divan and slowly walked over to her friend who was still in the euphoria of unbearable painful pleasure. Kat reached into their bag and removed a bottle of soothing cream, unbuckled the collar and wrist restraints, massaged cream into the redden skin on Jenna's wrists, then her neck. Jenna moaned under Kat's kneading. Standing up, she walked toward the attached bathroom, leaving Jenna on the bed, and ran a washcloth under warm water. There wasn't a bathtub in their attached bath, just a shower, and Kat thought about spending the extra money for the luxury she felt her friend needed. Walking back to her friend, who was nearly passed out, she began to sponge bathe Jenna's body, focusing on the open wounds on her back then helping her roll over to bathe the welts on her breasts.

Jenna's need was getting worse. It was nearly an addiction with the number of times a week that she needed a release. Kat rubbed the cloth between her friend's legs and examined her skin for any open wounds that would require a salts bath or first aid. After making sure Jenna was taken care of, Kat walked bath to the bathroom and deposited the soiled towel into the wash bin. She would need to talk to Jenna about her increasing cravings.

"Jenna?" Kat asked, brushing her friend's sweat-soaked curly hair from her face. "I need to get you dressed now. Then we can go to the bar and wait for Josh."

Jenna moaned and sat up as Kat placed the silver tunic over her friend's head and straightened the shirt. She then helped Jenna place both feet into her jeans and helped her stand up as she pulled the pants up over Jenna's thin hips.

"How the hell did you get these things buttoned?" Kat asked as she struggled with the button and zipper of Jenna's pants. Jenna giggled and pushed away her hands. She lay on the bed and pulled the ends together, first buttoning the jeans then zipping them up. Jenna lay still until Kat shook her again and helped her stand up.

"Come on. There's some bottled water in the mini fridge. We need to get out of here before they charge us double time," Kat said, helping Jenna to the little refrigerator near the chair that Kat sat in earlier. She handed Jenna the water and watched her friend's throat work as she quickly drank the entire bottle.

"Come on. Let's go babe."

Kat placed her arm around Jenna's waist just in case she needed support and the two of them walked back down the hall to the reception desk. Kat swiped her card again, signing out and they left through the door they entered more than an hour before.

The crowd was thinning out in the club area and Kat found two stools at the bar. She snagged them and helped Jenna into the seat before sitting in her own. Flagging down the bartender, she ordered Jenna another water and a shot of tequila for herself.

"Don't you ever get drunk?" Jenna asked as she sipped her water.

"You know I do. It was only a couple weeks ago that you had to hold my hair back as I hovered over the toilet."

Little Black Book

Jenna giggled and took another sip as a shot glass was placed in front of Kat. "How long do you think it's going to take Josh?" Jenna asked.

Kat shrugged her shoulders. "It depends on who was available for him tonight. He has his favorite and I know that he would pay extra to spend time with that one."

Their friend Josh was independently wealthy thanks to his father. Everyone knew that Josh was gay but dear old dad refused to admit it. Josh wasn't terribly flamboyant with his homosexuality, but the old man had to be completely obtuse to not realize.

Kat took a sip of her drink and looked up when a man approached them. He placed his hand on her shoulder and leaned down to talk in her ear. His head was smoothly shaved, bald, and his short bushy beard covered the lower part of his face. She looked up at him and sneered.

"I wouldn't. I don't date, I don't have sex, and I want nothing to do with you. You're wasting our time and asking for a throat punch."

EVILyn Reigns

"Oh, come on honey. I know I can change your mind. If not you then maybe your little friend. Or I could just take the both of you at the same time."

Kat could feel Jenna pull on her arm, but she was too late. Pulling back, she balled her fist and punched the man in his Adam's apple. She smiled as he began choking and bent over.

The bartender walked over. "Kat, you have got to stop punching my patrons. I'm trying to make money here and you keep chasing them away."

"Well, Bob, you need some patrons with better manners. When a woman says no, she means no."

The injured man wiped the tears from his eyes and looked at the bartender. "Are you going to do something, man? This bitch needs to be kicked out. She assaulted me," the bald man croaked.

The bartender shook his head. "Sorry, sir. She has priority status here. You can go, though. Kat, no more punching people. If someone is bothering you, come to me and I'll take care of it."

Little Black Book

Kat rolled her eyes and took another sip of her drink as the other man stormed off. "Great, Kat. You owe me his tip," the bartender stated, disappointed.

"I doubt he tipped much anyway. Just another small dick with big dick energy," she said as she pulled a twenty from her vest pocket and placed it in the tip jar. "That should cover anyone else I need to punch tonight."

The bartender shook his head and walked away to attend to someone else at the bar.

"You're going to get arrested someday," Jenna said as she leaned against Kat.

"I doubt it. I only maim the assholes of society."

Jenna snickered and turned as Josh joined them at the bar. "What's shaken, bacon?" he asked as he sat down. Kat heard him order another Bloody Mary and she shook her head.

"What took you so long, J?" Kat asked.

EVILyn Reigns

"One of my favorites was working tonight and I asked him for the special. I may not be able to sit or walk correctly for a week."

Kat rolled her eyes as he and Jenna laughed together. It was going to be a long night.

•

"Daddy! Stop please."

The rips of fabric echoed in the small bedroom as the young girl began to struggle against the abrasive hands tearing at her pale skin.

"Daddy! No!"

Dozens of faces filled her teary vision as she felt the violation of her innocence. She closed her eyes against the onslaught of violence, hiding in the recesses of her mind until the assault finally ended. Her battered body lay still as the last man climbed off her. She lay, her vision empty, her mind gone as the door closed. Why did they hurt her. Why did her daddy let them hurt her? Seconds later her bedroom door opened to her father standing in the entry.

Little Black Book

"Daddy why?" she whispered. She closed her eyes when he began to remove his belt. The lashes removed her flesh with the sound of the belt hitting her skin. Her cries filled the room until she finally succumbed to the darkness.

Kat woke with a start, remnants of the nightmare giving her waking mind cobwebs. She breathed heavily as she wiped the tears and sweat from her face, her hair soaked through and hanging down her back.

Echoes of her traumatic childhood spun through her mind, exposing every single moment that shamed her. Pain filled her temples with the beginning of a migraine, and she leaned over to her nightstand, blindly searching for her medicine. The tequila from yesterday evening combined with their bondage play did not help Kat's nightmares. They seemed to be getting worse. No matter how hard Kat tried to move on with her life, the trauma of her childhood chased her. She lost the ability to trust any man, her capacity to feel an orgasm with another person forever ruined with the quick thrusts that ended her innocence and childhood forever.

Standing from the bed, she stretched her arms over her head and walked toward the shower, hoping the steaming hot water would clear the beginnings of her migraine and wash the sins from her soul. Kat climbed into the stall and stood under the punishing, scalding steam. Memories of her childhood played like a reel through her mind as she rested her head against the shower wall, relishing in the heat as it scalded her skin.

She laughed to herself. Childhood. What childhood? After Kat's mother died, her father turned to drugs. As a child, she never knew or even understood the concept of drugs. Soon, her mother's estate ran out of money and her father turned toward something even more reprehensible and illegal. He sold his daughter to the drug dealers.

Kat turned off the shower and dried her body before she hung the towel over the shower rod. She wiped the steam from the mirror and stared at her reflection. Demons invaded her mind, telling her how ugly she was, how soulless it was that she would sell her body. The scars across her face stood out in the dim yellow bathroom light and she tried to forget the day she received them. The day that Kathy died, and Kat was born.

Walking back to the bedroom, Kat began to get dressed. She pulled a large black shirt on over her head and a pair of small biker shorts went up over her hips. She grabbed her laundry basket and walked toward the laundry room in her apartment. Laundry closet, really. Kat began to sort through her clothes when a knock on her door interrupted her chore. She gave her door a dirty look. She knew exactly who was visiting her this early on a Saturday morning.

The front door swung open, Josh and Jenna walking in, calling her name.

"I'm doing laundry," she yelled, shaking her head, and trying to hide her smile before Josh found her. "You're supposed to only use my key for emergencies. Laundry day is not an emergency," Kat said as she continued to sort her clothes.

EVILyn Reigns

"It is totally an emergency if you're wearing that hideous thing. Get dressed, we're going sailing," Josh said as he took a pair of shorts from her and threw them back into the basket.

"I am not going to go sailing. We're in San Antonio. There's nowhere to sail around here. It's also hot as Hades out. Go away."

"No way, chica. We're going to go sailing. My dad just bought a new sailboat and hired the cutest sailor captain to work it. I'm going to work my indescribable gay boy charms on him and get married, live happily ever after, and adopt a dozen kids. I need a wing woman." He leaned over and took away another item of clothing from her hands and started to throw them in the basket. Kat grabbed them back and they began a gentle tug of war.

Jenna began to laugh hysterically, falling against the wall and sliding down to the floor, holding her stomach.

"What the hell is so funny?" Kat asked as she turned toward her friend.

Little Black Book

Jenna hiccupped and wiped tears from her eyes. "You and 'Gay Boy Josh' are fighting over a pair of panties. I thought I'd never see the day that Josh would want to get into a girl's panties."

Josh immediately dropped the thong and turned toward Jenna, hip cocked. He shook his finger. "First of all, I'm not trying to get into her panties. I'm trying to get her to drop her panties."

Both Kat and Jenna began to laugh,

"Shut up you hookers!" Josh squealed. "I give up. I'm packing your bag, Kat. We are going to Corpus Christi to go sailing and that's final. I called the library and I know you don't have to go back to work until Tuesday, so for the next two days, you're mine. You can do your laundry when you get back."

Josh stormed out of the room while the women laughed. Kat wiped a humorous tear from her face and shook her head. "Oh God, I needed that."

"Me too," Jenna said as she stood up from the floor.

Kat brushed a stray curl from Jenna's face. "Are you okay?"

EVILyn Reigns

Her friend nodded. "I feel great. I am recharged. Thank you."

Kat nodded. "I better go kick Josh out of my closet before he has me looking like a Carmen Miranda."

Chapter 5

Closing the front door behind her, Kat dropped her duffel bag to the floor and shuffled over to her couch, collapsing onto the cushions. She winced as she rubbed her shoulders. Removing her shirt, she examined her pinkened skin and hissed as she tried to lower her bra straps. Kat definitely didn't put on enough sunblock while they were out on the boat, giggling as she remembered Josh's antics to gain the attention of the sailboat captain.

EVILyn Reigns

Unfortunately for her friend, he was more interested in Jenna than Josh.

Kat laid on the boat and watched as Josh and Jenna took turns strutting near the sailboat pilot, showing off their best moves, both disappointed that he wouldn't act on their flirtations. After a full day of sailing, and all three of them tipsy from the canned wine, they went back to the hotel to crash. Personally, if she had to hear Josh whine one more time about his dad's sexy boat captain, she was going to take her belt to Josh's backside.

No, probably not, he would enjoy it too much, she thought.

Kat huffed and removed herself from the couch, wincing as her burned skin stuck to the leather. She had a lot of laundry to do and also needed to recover for her library shift the next day. As she finished sorting the clothes that Josh interrupted two days before, she began to reminisce on the weekend and how she didn't have a single nightmare. Kat shared a king size hotel bed with both Josh and Jenna, not sexually of course, but maybe just having someone in her bed helped drive her demons away.

Throwing a load of clothes into the washer, Kat added some soap and started the wash. She then walked back to her room and lay on her bed to stare at the ceiling. Lately, the nightmares from her past had been getting worse and she wasn't sure why. Her father died long ago, leaving her with a large life insurance check. Kat was going to donate the entire windfall, but Jenna talked her out of that decision. Just because the money was tainted with her own blood didn't mean she shouldn't spend it. Her father's insurance was in the millions, even more so now that the majority of it had been invested.

Rolling onto her side, Kat stared out the window, her mind driving a hundred miles an hour. She didn't need to work, but if she didn't, Kat would go crazy with boredom. She also loved the library and the solace it provided her. The small apartment was perfect for her, and the inheritance money helped fund the illicit lifestyles that she and Jenna secretly lived.

EVILyn Reigns

Kat knew why she was the way she was. Her life at the hands of her abusers shaped her into the perverted person she was today. She couldn't have sex. She needed to watch others in order to orgasm. Kat also couldn't stand to be touched by a lover but inflicting pain onto others gave her a euphoria that could never be explained. Some days, when she needed her release, she felt like there was something wrong with her.

Jenna was her friend and perfect partner because she loved sex, especially with strangers, but she couldn't orgasm unless she was in pain. Kat didn't trust anyone else to help them achieve their high, so they relied on one other, both promising that if they needed to chase that particular fetish, they would turn to only each other. Kat wasn't sure why Jenna needed to be in pain, and her friend refused to talk about her childhood, same as Kat. But whatever it was that shaped Jenna into who she was, they probably deserved death.

Little Black Book

Just like Kat's father deserved his death. Her eyelids grew heavy as she slowly drifted into an exhausted sleep.

•

Kathy hurriedly packed a backpack and rushed around her room, gathering any mementoes that she didn't think she could live without. The silver picture frame of her mother went in her bag along with the roll of cash that she had been secretly stashing behind her father's back. She was finally 18 and had been counting down the days until her birthday. She would finally be free from the abuse that she had suffered under her father's hand since she was a little girl.

Kathy rubbed the bruise under her arm and winced in pain as she threw the backpack over her shoulders and ran through the house toward the back door. She wasn't sure where she was going to go, or what she was going to do when she got there. All she knew was that she had to leave before he killed her. Last week he sold her for the last time. When the man climbed off her body, she lay on the bed, bleeding from several areas, pain no longer registering in her mind. She thought about taking a knife to her wrists. There was no other way to escape her fate.

The thought of suicide was fleeting, then anger colored her vision. He was supposed to be her father. Dads are supposed to protect their children. Instead, her father did the opposite. Protect wasn't a word that he knew. Kathy had to get herself out. She only had herself to rely on and she vowed right then as she lay cowered in a fetal position, she would protect herself. Maybe someday she could even get revenge.

Kathy made it to the kitchen and opened the back door. A heavy shadow fell over her as the door was yanked out from her hand and slammed closed, then her body was thrown across the kitchen floor and she felt her head hit the wall, hard. "Where do you think you're going?"

Looking up, she saw her father standing over her as he cracked his knuckles. She winced and cowered as he crossed his arms over his burly chest.

Little Black Book

"You're not going anywhere, not for a very long time," he said as he began to remove his belt.

"Why? Why do you hurt me? Why do you let other men hurt me? You're supposed to be my father. Fathers protect their daughter,." Kathy said as she began to cry.

"Pshh... You're not my daughter. Your mother died and I was stuck with you. You were her brat, but you were never my child. I might as well make a penny and get some enjoyment from you though. You're a better fuck than your momma ever was."

Kathy screamed out as he lifted her from the floor and threw her over the counter, unbuckling his pants and yanking her leggings down. As he kicked her legs apart and thrust into her from behind, she cried out in pain and frustration. Kathy promised herself this would never happen again and here she was, still a victim. The counter dug into her pelvis rhythmically as he grunted behind her, pulling her hair. He pushed her head down on the counter, hard, and she screamed at the pain that exploded in her *face. He had one hand on the counter that held him up and a red haze came over her. She didn't think, just turned her head to the other side and bit down on his wrist as hard as she could, gagging as the metallic iron taste of blood filled her mouth.*

"You bitch!" he yelled as he fell backward off her body and on the floor. She lay still for a moment on the counter, staring at the blood that pooled under her face. Kathy lifted her head and stared at the large bloody salad serving fork that was on the counter. She touched her face and winced at the long grooves that were cut into her skin. The repetition of her body being shoved against the counter and the fork driving into her face with every thrust created long grooves in her cheek that bled freely.

Her father's hand grabbed her hair and pulled her up from the counter. He began to rain down blows on her face as she screamed from his massive fists hitting her already injured cheek. Kathy reached behind her and feeling the fork, she grasped it. Before he could hit her again, she jammed the fork as hard as she could into his neck and backed away as quickly as she could, falling when she tripped over her leggings that were around her knees.

Kathy lay on the floor and watched as the man she thought was her father fell, gurgling as blood began to bubble out of his mouth. He tried to reach for the utensil sticking out of his neck before his hand fell aside and more blood from his neck pooled underneath him. She stood up as gingerly as she could, pulled her pants up, and tiptoed over to the now prone body. Kat checked his pulse and squeaked when she couldn't feel any evidence of his heart beating.

She killed her father.

He was never her father.

Kathy rushed over to her backpack, picked it up and began to walk out the back door. She was free. Revenge was hers. She would never let anyone hurt her again.

Kathy died and beginning today, she was only Kat.

●

EVILyn Reigns

The washer buzzer was overwhelmingly loud as she sat up from her bed, covered in sweat. It figured that she didn't have any nightmares for a few days and then has the worst one yet. Kat stood up from the bed and stretched her arms over her head, groaning as her back cracked. She walked over to her washer and moved her clothes into the dryer. Her stomach growled and she walked over to the refrigerator to see if there was any leftover Chinese from when Josh visited last. Kat pulled out the kung pow chicken and sniffed it, shrugged, then grabbed a fork and began to eat. Maybe she'd invite Jenna over to sleep so she wouldn't have another nightmare.

Kat wasn't sure why the memories kept overwhelming her mind. There might be something her subconscious was telling her. No one ever found out that she was the one that killed her father, well, the man she thought was her father. She was so worried about prison that Kat disappeared as quickly as she could. It wasn't until she enrolled into college that the insurance company caught up with her to award Kat death benefits. She decided that donating the entire amount was the way to go. It felt like blood money, her blood. When Jenna found out Kat's plan with the money and why she wanted to get rid of it, her friend talked her into keeping it and investing it. At the end of the day, it was a great decision since she was able to provide her and Jenna with the eclectic lifestyle they enjoyed.

 Wrinkling her nose at the bitter taste of the chicken, Kat threw out her food and walked back to her bedroom to get dressed. She might as well go to the grocery store and stock up for the week. As she was getting dressed, she heard her phone alerting her to a text. Kat smiled as she read Jenna's message. It looked as though this day wasn't a waste after all. "Fun first, groceries second," she said to herself as she slipped on her ripped jeans and leather vest. Kat packed a duffle bag with some personal items before leaving her apartment to drive to Jenna's.

•

 The knock on the door echoed in the hallway of the apartment as Kat waited for the door to unlock

EVILyn Reigns

and open. Kat walked into the apartment, kicking the door shut behind her. She locked the door and walked back toward Jenna's bedroom, expecting her friend to follow her.

"How much do we need tonight?" Kat asked when she felt Jenna standing closely behind her.

"It's not too bad right now. But I do need some help."

"Do I need to call him?" Kat asked referring to their regular that joined their sessions at S & P.

"No, let's keep it between us."

Kat nodded and motioned toward the bed as she ruffled through her backpack to remove some of the toys that she brought along. She watched Jenna's expression as she pulled out a pair of nipple clamps, a large anal plug, and a small bullet vibrator that was attached to a remote. Jenna began shaking her head and smiling. "What?" Kat asked.

Jenna giggled. "I was just wondering if you're the Mary Poppins of sex toys. What else are you going to pull out of your magic bag? A sex swing?"

Little Black Book

Kat smiled. "I left that in my other purse." Both women laughed together before Kat dropped her smile and motioned for Jenna to undress and lay on the bed. "Do you remember the code words?"

Jenna nodded. "Pineapple to slow down. Apple to stop."

"Good girl," Kat replied as she began to pull thick scarves from her backpack. She smiled, thinking of their earlier joke about her bag. She tied the long scarves around the legs at the head of the bed and waited patiently as Jenna removed her clothes and laid naked on top of the bedspread. Kat quietly tied the scarves around Jenna's wrists and removed the nipple clamps from the box. She leaned over the bed and blew cool air onto Jenna's now erect nipples. Kat pinched one nipple, smiling as she heard Jenna squeak, and fastened the clamp onto the deep brown nipple. She had to suck on the second nipple in order to get it erect enough, and repeated the process, relishing in Jenna's moans. Kat then walked over to her friend's closet to remove her favorite riding crop. She walked back to the bed and laid the crop next to Jenna before picking up the butt plug from the nightstand, slathering it with warming oil.

"Lift your knees and pick up your hips."

Kat watched Jenna struggle to perform the demand with her wrists tied to the bed. Kat climbed into the bed and grabbed one leg, lifting it to rest on her own shoulder before she lined the plug up to Jenna's back entrance. She poured warming oil all over Jenna and watched as it flowed from her clit to her anus, pooling onto the bed underneath. Kat slowly pushed the plug into Jenna's ass as her friend moaned at the pleasure from the invasion. As the plug became seated deep inside Jenna, Kat sat away from her friend, and she slowly lowered the leg she was holding and picked up the leather crop that lay on the bed.

Rubbing the leather tip of the crop against Jenna's clit, Kat stood up next to the bed, spurred on by the constant moaning from her lover. Raising the crop, Kat began to bestow light lashes to Jenna's naked torso, striking her breasts and stomach, leaving behind light pink welts that adorned her dark skin.

When Jenna began to writhe on the bed, moaning uncontrollably, Kat sat the crop down on the bedspread and lifted the remote-controlled bullet vibrator. She sat on the bed next to Jenna and pulled her friend's leg back, separating the lower lips of her vagina, relishing in the liquid that poured from its source that spread between Jenna's thighs. She placed the vibrator at Jenna's moist opening and pushed it slowly inside, eliciting an orgasmic scream.

"I need you to turn over, now!" Kat demanded and waited as Jenna struggled with her bonds to turn onto her belly on the bed. She screamed as she lay relaxed on her stomach and Kat smiled as she remembered the nipple clamps. Kat picked up the crop and slowly traced the muscles in Jenna's back before she made the first strike. She began to whip Jenna's back in time with the harmonious moans that echoed around the small bedroom. Jenna writhed, screamed, and moaned with every welt Kat left behind on her skin before she stiffened, squealing as if she was dying a slow death.

Kat lay next to Jenna in bed, dropping the crop onto the floor, and reached her hand into her pants. She flicked her own clit along with the sounds of Jenna's moans, the buzzing of her friend's vibrator spurring her own orgasm that rose into her body. Her hips bucked against her own hand, the growls and moans that escaped her mouth overshadowing Jenna's quiet cries.

"Pineapple. Pineapple," Jenna whispered.

Kat stood up from the bed and picked up the remote, turning off the vibrator. Jenna lay almost comatose on the bed, unable to move from their session. Kat removed the anal plug and took it to the bathroom, placing it in the sink to clean later. She returned to the bedroom and helped Jenna roll over and sit up.

"This might hurt," Kat said as she gently removed the first nipple clamp.

Jenna hissed, trying to lean away from Kat as she reached for the second clamp, gently releasing, and removing the painful metal. Kat wiped a painful tear from Jenna's face, helped her friend stand up, and half carried her toward the bathroom, assisting her into the tub before she turned on the hot water. Jenna looked up at her in reverence, surprising Kat.

"Kat, thank you so much. Thank you."

Kat nodded and began to help her friend bathe, steam filling the small bathroom. She didn't know if it was the steam or her tears that obscured her vision as she gently bathed her friend.

EVILyn Reigns

Chapter 6

The absence of sound seemed to echo in the library as Kat sat at her desk, playing solitaire on her computer. Wednesdays always seemed to be the slowest day of the week. Maybe she should close the library a little early and head home for a microwave dinner and Netflix. Kat usually got in trouble when she closed up early, but she didn't care. It's not as if she needed the job and sitting around all day and watching time move so slowly was going to make her go psycho. Deciding to close, she stood up and began

EVILyn Reigns

to shut her computer system down. The bell above the library door jingled and she looked up sharply, disgruntled that her plan for an early night was interrupted. A large, bald man with a bushy beard that covered half of his face strolled up toward the desk where she stood. She couldn't tell if he was handsome or not under his beard, but his eyes looked very familiar, and she tilted her head as she tried to place where she had seen him before. "Hello, how may I help you?" Kat asked as he stood behind the desk.

"You don't remember me, do you?" the man asked as he rubbed the beard on his face.

Kat shook her head. "I'm sorry. I don't. Can I help you find a book?"

"Yeah, I'm looking for a 'how to' book. How to get you to go out with me without you assaulting me."

Kat's eyes widened as she remembered where she saw him. This was the jerk from the club last week. She stood to her full height plus the four inches her Jimmy Choo's allowed and walked around the counter toward the man, smirking as he stepped back. He was over a foot taller than her and seemed to fear what she may do.

"I don't date. I don't entertain assholes that are rude to me and my friends. I don't have sex. All you are doing is wasting the oxygen in this building and asking for me to yank your esophagus out through your neck. Now, unless you need help finding an actual book, I suggest you leave."

The man rubbed the top of his bald head. "Look, we got off on the wrong foot. I was a little drunk and I can get belligerent. You're just so beautiful and I want to get to know you."

"Buddy, I already know you. Now, I don't want to help you at all. Leave," Kat said as she began to walk toward the front door. As soon as she threw this guy out, she was going to lock up for the night. She stopped as he grabbed her arm. Kat looked pointedly at his hand on her skin before he snatched away his hand and backed up a step.

"Look, you don't know me. You don't even know my name. At least give me a chance."

EVILyn Reigns

Looking up at the security cameras, Kat wondered if she would get fired for getting blood all over the floor. She rolled her eyes and stepped closer to her 'admirer.'

"Okay, let's play. I do know everything there is worth knowing about you. I bet you tip ten percent on tickets if the service was good, but mostly you stiff the wait staff every time. In fact, I bet you find something wrong with the food so you can get it for free because you can't afford a nice meal with your minimum wage job shoveling shit at the equestrian center. You like to date blondes but prefer redheads, but you chase away every woman that was ever interested in you when you prove that your ham hock hands do your talking for you, especially when you drink. You can't hold your liquor and become a whiny pussy when things don't go your way. You probably even have a basic white boy name and grow that monstrosity beard to hide your itty-bitty chin and thin as toothpick lips. Let me guess. You're a Chad."

Little Black Book

Kat smiled and nodded as his eyes widened when she guessed his name.

"You have a record of bar fights but you possibly have a family member or a buddy in law enforcement that keeps bailing you out so you don't get stuck in a Texas prison because of the three strike law. You think that you have what it takes to keep a woman satisfied but you have a stiff tongue and a loose dick. Oh, and you're also an Aries with an April birthday. In fact, I'd wager my left boob that you were born on Easter and your mommy thought you were something special until she discovered your mean temper and pulled you off her tit. Now, if you will please follow me to the door, the library is now closed and if you need any assistance in finding a book, I suggest that you go on Amazon."

Kat's heels clicked along the marble floor as she walked toward the entrance and held the door open for the man as he stood stunned in front of her desk, his mouth open in shock.

"We don't need a fly catcher, 'Chad.' Close your mouth and head on home."

EVILyn Reigns

He closed his mouth and stomped toward the door. "You're going to regret this, you bitch."

"Oh, I already do, 'Chad.'"

He turned to face her at the door. "You got one thing wrong. My name is not Chad; it's Kyle."

"Same difference, 'Chad,'" Kat said as she slammed the door shut on his stunned face and twisted the lock, satisfied with the loud click. She heaved a sigh and walked back toward her desk. "Ugh, men," Kat whispered as she gathered her purse and backpack. Maybe she needed to go to the gym tonight and work off some steam. She picked up her phone and sent a text to Joshua. He loved going to the gym with her but hated working out. Not ideal, but better than nothing.

•

Thuds echoed in the small gym as Kat hit the heavy punching bag. Boxing gloves protected her fists and sweat beaded on her upper lip as she worked out her frustrations. She noticed Josh watching another boxer in the gym and not paying attention to her. She spun and thumped the bag with a roundhouse kick, aiming for his head.

"Jesus Christ on a cracker, Kat! That almost got me right in the face!" Josh yelled as he ducked. He blushed as everyone in the gym turned to stare at them.

"Stop drooling over all your future daddies and pay attention. Hold the fucking bag."

"Jesus, you're in a temper." Josh repositioned himself behind the bag and she gleefully resumed punching, smiling with his every wince. "You get off on this shit, don't you?" Josh asked as he rolled his shoulders.

Kat shrugged and pointed to herself with her boxing glove. "Masochist."

Holding out her fists for Josh to remove her tape, she took a deep breath, wrinkling her nose at the sweaty gym smell that invaded her senses.

"I'm going to go hit the showers. Can you be lookout?" Kat asked as she walked toward the locker room in the back of the gym. She loved to visit KO Zone, a boxing gym that catered to only men. Well, only men until she came along. Unfortunately, they hadn't added a women's locker room just for little ole her so she always brought Josh or Jenna to be her lookout while she showered and changed. Kat had been taking boxing lessons and Krav Maga since college. She vowed to herself that she would never be a victim again and decided to best way to assure her promise was to take classes that would allow her to protect herself. It was during a sparring lesson when she drew blood on her opponent during a Krav Maga fight that she discovered her kink. She grew heated with desire with every punch and kick that she landed. It wasn't too much longer after that she and Jenna discovered each other's kinks and decided to help each other out.

  Kat walked out of the locker room, refreshed, and wrapped her arm around Joshua's waist, pulling his attention away from the sweaty half naked men in the boxing ring.

  "You're lucky that you're my bestie, bitch," he whined as they walked out of the gym.

Little Black Book

"Should we go out for dinner tonight?" Kat asked as they walked toward her brown Buick.

Josh nodded. "Yeah, I'll text Jenna and see if she has the night off. If not, we could bug her at Garnet Embrace."

Kat rolled her eyes as Josh began to text their friend. She wasn't dressed for the club. Her tight jeans and Jimmy Choo's might get swiped by the strippers working the pole at the club. She climbed into the driver's seat of her car and waited as Josh finished texting so he could tell her where they were going.

"Well?" she asked.

"Head to Garnet. Jenna said she was talked into a shift. We can grab some hot wings there while we wait for our girl to get off."

Kat rolled her eyes again before starting the car and driving off toward the club. The food there was okay, but she was getting tired of the strippers hitting on her.

•

EVILyn Reigns

Music pumped through her veins as Kat sat at a table in front of the stage. Oil stains covered the wood flooring under the pole and the smell of sweaty desperation had her wrinkling her nose in disgust. Jenna walked up to the table and slid a basket of wings in front of her and Josh. Jenna sat in the seat next to Kat and picked up a hot wing, nibbling on the spicy chicken.

"Aren't you supposed to be working?" Kat asked as she took her wing back from Jenna.

"It's Wednesday night, our slowest night of the week. The regulars in here don't tip for shit and I am hungry," Jenna answered as she swiped the wing away from Kat.

"Well, then why are you here working? Duck out and let's go get some real food somewhere," Josh stated as he swiped Jenna's wing before she could bite into it.

"Will you two bitches quit stealing my food!" Jenna cried out as she grabbed another wing from the basket.

Little Black Book

Kat giggled and took the wing from Jenna again before she could bite into it. "It's my food. I'm paying for it, and you're supposed to be working, not filching your customer's food."

As the evening wore on and Jenna was called away to bartend and serve food, more women began to walk into the bar. Kat looked around shocked at the tables and booths that held about a dozen women scantily dressed in heavy makeup. One woman wore nothing but a black suit jacket and black heels, her blonde hair styled and curled around her head like a lion's mane. Jenna slid into the chair next to Kat and took a drink of her soda before she swiped another French fry.

"Jenna, what is going on tonight? What's with all the women in the club? There's not that many men here tonight. I thought I heard you say that it was your slowest night of the week?"

Her friend giggled and stood up, backing away from their table. "Our manager is looking to hire a few more dancers and she decided to hold an amateur night to see the local talent. Oh, and I signed you up. I hope you have skills."

Kat quickly stood up and grabbed at her friend, screeching at Jenna. "How dare you! Ugh! I can't strip on stage!"

"Looks like it's going to be a fun night after all!" Josh said as he sat back in his chair and crossed his arms."

"I wouldn't look too smug, 'Gay Boy Josh.' I signed you up for a dance too. And so, you two don't feel left out, I signed myself up as well," Jenna said laughing before she walked away to the back room.

Kat and Josh stared at each other in shock. "I don't think I can do this," she said.

"I don't know why you're complaining. I am a gay man about to strip for a bunch of women. I'm going to get booed!"

The lights lowered in the club and an announcer began to introduce Jenna over the loudspeaker. Nicki Minaj and Chainz began to flood the silent room as Jenna walked out on stage.

"Cute," Kat said as she swayed along with the music and clapped to the beat as Jenna began to dance on the darkened stage. A spotlight lit up her friend's body as she jumped onto the pole, wrapping one leg around the bar. She spun around as she leaned her head back, her dark curls fanning out with the speed of the spin.

"If we're going to do this, we better do this right," Kat said to Josh as she began to dig into her purse for money. He began to follow suit and Kat walked over to the edge of the stage to slide money into Jenna's thong. Change was thrown onto the stage next to Jenna and Kat looked over at Josh.

"Really? Quarters?" Kat asked as she shoved him.

"Hey, I'm making her work for it," he said.

Kat giggled as Jenna danced over to Josh and began to gyrate in front of his face before she crawled onto all fours and sat up on her knees. She grabbed Josh's head and pushed his face in between her breasts before she slid backwards and presented the side of her thong to him.

EVILyn Reigns

"Okay, if I wasn't totally gay, that would have been hot," he gasped as he slid a hundred-dollar bill into Jenna's thong.

Kat laughed and clapped along to the song before the music faded away and Jenna strutted off the stage.

"I don't know why you're smiling," Josh said when the lights brightened. "Jenna told me that you were next, and she chose your song. You're dancing to "My Humps."

Kat laughed and pushed Josh out of her way. "Bring it on, bitches. I'm ready to show off my ass!"

Chapter 7

Kat's groan split the air as she woke from a deep sleep. Their amateur night turned into one of her best nights. She had so much fun, but her muscles ached so much. Kat couldn't remember the last time she worked out so much in one evening. She smiled as she remembered Josh dancing to "It's Raining Men." It was a good thing he wasn't dependent on stripping or tips because he was the worst dancer she had ever seen. Not only did he not have any rhythm, but he kept slipping and sliding on the body oil left behind on the floor.

Kat shook her head and tried to get out of bed so she could get ready for work. "Nope," she said as her muscles screamed in protest. Kat grabbed her cellphone from her nightstand and sent a text to her boss at the library. There was no way she could even think about standing on her feet let alone trying to restock heavy books. Her eyes drifted close as she relaxed in her bed.

"Yes, a nap sounds good indeed," she said to herself as she fell back to sleep.

•

Kat woke with start, sitting straight up. She wiped the sweat from her face. Her body spasmed from the nightmare and her nightclothes were soaked through. She had another dream from her childhood, the father she thought she had selling her to the worst of the worst. Kat ran her hand through her sweat-soaked hair and blew out a breath. One would think that her terrors would finally go away. Her father had been dead for years.

Shrugging her sore shoulders, Kat stood up and stretched before she made her way to the bathroom. Her eyes caught the clock on her wall, and she smiled. It was close to 6 p.m. and she had slept the day away. The three of them were supposed to go to Strokers & Pokers tonight. Kat rubbed her hands together with anticipation. It had only been a couple of days but she could never get enough of the intimacy that she experienced with Jenna.

Kat finished up in the shower and began to dress as a pounding knock boomed on the front door of her apartment. She looked toward the door in shock, wondering who it could be. Jenna and Josh usually just walked in. She hoped it wasn't the creep that had been following her around.

Throwing on a long robe, Kat walked toward the door and opened it, surprised to see Josh standing at the door, tears staining his cheeks.

"Oh, God. Josh. What is it?" she asked as she pulled him into her apartment.

"Kat, I don't know how to tell you this. I don't even know what to say."

"Josh, stop it. You're scaring me."

He began to pace in her living room, running his hand through his blue tipped hair. "Kat... It's Jenna."

"What's wrong. Oh my God! Josh what happened. Spit it out."

He took both of Kat's hands in his and held tightly. "I went over to her apartment this morning to tease her about yesterday. She was... She was.... Oh, I can't even say it out loud." He paused, gulping down air before blurting, "Kat, Jenna was murdered last night."

She shook her head. "No, you're wrong. Is this a joke? It's not funny." Kat tried to pull her hands away from Josh.

"Kat, it's not a joke. I found her early this morning. She was tied up, beaten, raped. I have been at the police station all day. I'm sorry, Kat."

She pulled her hands out of his hands and pushed him away. "You're lying. Don't lie to me."

Kat burrowed her face in her hands as Josh wrapped his arms around her.

"I'm so sorry Kat."

The room swirled around Kat as she fell to the floor, bringing Josh with her when he couldn't hold her up. Heaving sobs poured from her chest before she let out screams of pain, of heartbreak. They sat on the floor together, their souls shattered, as they mourned the loss of their family.

•

Kat and Josh stood at the gravestone in the cemetery all alone. Jenna didn't have family, never talked about her family either, so they stood together, alone. A single tear escaped Kat's eye as she placed a single rose and kiss on the cold cement that now forever held her heart. Josh laid his hands on her shoulders, gave her a squeeze, and tried to turn her away from the gravestone.

"I'm not ready yet," she said, shrugging his hands from her cold skin. She felt as if she would always be cold, that warm was a temperature that was forever lost.

"Kat, we need to leave. It's getting late and we should leave. The caretakers are waiting for us so they can close the cemetery."

She shook her head and dropped to her knees, cold wet mud from the grass seeping into her black tights. Kat tried to hold the overwhelming emotions inside, but she broke at the thought of leaving Jenna alone in the dark.

"Go ahead and leave. I'm fine here."

"Kat..."

She shook her head again and hiccupped. "Not now Josh."

Wiping the tears from her eyes, she pulled a piece of paper from her jumper pocket. "I debated reading you my thoughts, Jen. We both know how fucked up I am. But since it's only me and Josh here, I figured it was okay. I won't be whole without you. What am I supposed to do now? The dreams are getting worse. My cravings are getting worse.

Little Black Book

"Poet Alfred Lord Tennyson coined the phrase, *'It is better to have loved and lost than never to have loved at all.'*

"No offense to Tennyson, but this hurts so much. I wonder if people would be better off not loving anyone at all. The over encompassing pain that surrounds my heart won't allow the appreciating emotion of knowing such a beautiful creature that drifted in and out of my life. I created a poem that might help express that feeling.

"The wind blows by me.
I can feel you touch my face on the breeze.
You will forever follow the path that you loved
Along the beaches of your favorite sea.

We watch the children play,
And people live their lives day after day
Naive of the pain we feel.
Oh God, please make it go away.

I watch you in the waves,

EVILyn Reigns

Such a torrent and miraculous display.
You will stay alive in our hearts.
Our love for you will never be contained.

"After thinking on my life with Jenna, I decided that I would feel this pain in my heart for the rest of my life for just five seconds of her smile than to never have met her. Maybe Tennyson had it right. We have loved. We have lost. But she will still live on forever.

"In our hearts,

"In our memories,

"In our dreams.

"Were you truly murdered, or did you go to an outsider for your needs and things got carried away? I wish you would have called me. I would have been there for you.

"I will forever be empty without you." Kat folded the letter and placed it on the gravestone before turning away and allowing Josh to enfold her in his arms. He rubbed her back and nuzzled the top of her head with his chin.

Little Black Book

"Hey Kat?"

"Yeah?"

"That poem was terrible."

She smiled and giggled as she slapped him on the back. "Shut up, Josh." The two of them walked back to her car as they held one another in each other's arms.

EVILyn Reigns

Chapter 8

Three months later

Kat stared at the wall in her apartment as she sat on her couch, the television blaring in the background. It had been three months since she lost the love of her life. Jenna was more than just a friend. She was everything to Kat and without the beacon of love that accompanied Jenna, Kat had found herself without the motivation to live. She lost her job shortly after Jenna's death because she stopped showing up to the library. Kat couldn't even imagine doing anything other than slowly dying on her couch as time marched by her window.

Kat hmphed. It seemed no matter how much she tried to waste away, Josh would show up with what used to be her favorite food, Kung Pow Chicken. She thought about taking her own life several times but chickened out every time she gave one of her knives a dirty look. Today was another dull day in her dull life without the color that Jenna used to provide. Her front door opened, Josh walking in with a bag of Mexican takeout.

"Honey, I'm home."

"Go away, Josh," Kat said as she lay back down on the couch. She secretly watched as he placed the food on the table and walked back out the door. A few seconds later, he came back into her apartment holding a medium sized box.

"I thought today would be a good day to go over her things. We could do it together while we eat disgusting cheesy Mexican and maybe get drunk on some sour wine."

"I'm not sure if I'm ready."

Little Black Book

Josh shook his head. "We can do this together." He walked over and placed the box on the floor in front of the couch. "God dang, that television is loud." Josh grabbed the remote and turned off the device.

Kat reached down and pulled a flap of the box up, peeking inside. "What is this?"

"I was cleaning out her apartment and I found this box under her bed. Most of her clothes and belongings were donated to a shelter here in San Antonio. I found a few things in her closet that I thought you might like to look through, so I placed them in the box as well."

She watched Josh walk back toward the kitchen and listened to him as he puttered around in the other room. Kat opened the medium-sized box and began to look through it, tears welling up in her eyes as she fingered through their memories. Old movie tickets, pictures, and a keychain lay in the box. Kat fingered the keychain, a photo of all three of them on St. Patrick's, decked out in green, wearing the green shamrock headbands that Josh forced onto their heads. She heard Josh clearing his throat and looked up from the trinket in her hand.

"What did you find there?"

Kat swallowed the lump in her throat. "A keychain. It's a picture of us from last year during Saint Patrick's Day. We got so drunk on Guinness and then you forced us to wear these ridiculous headbands. We bar hopped all night and passed out at your dad's house. Do you remember his expression when he found the three of us in our green panties wearing nothing else but those stupid headbands?"

Josh laughed and took a seat next to Kat on the couch. "Yeah, I remember. My dad was ecstatic. He thought I had a threesome. Hell, the three of us were so drunk, we could have very well had a threesome and not remembered it. And I'll have you know that my panties were very manly."

"You were wearing my panties, dipshit."

They both laughed and dug through the box. Josh left the room and quickly returned with two margaritas and an order of quesadillas. The two of

Little Black Book

them laughed and cried as they went through Jenna's box. Kat wasn't sure how many margaritas she drank or how strong Josh was making them, but they were both very drunk when Kat pulled out a small black book.

"What's that?" he asked, taking the book from her hand. Kat snatched the book back and flipped through it as she drank her concoction.

"I think this is a journal of some kind. It's in Jenna's handwriting anyway, but it's not a journal like I've ever seen. Here, what do you make of it?" Kat said as she passed the small book back to Josh.

He read a few lines and looked up sharply, surprise etched into his face. "I think this is a keeping of clients. I know Jenna bartended and waitressed for that strip club, but I didn't think she did personal dances, did she?"

"No, she told me that they wouldn't let her because she wasn't the 'right type of woman' they wanted for their club."

"You mean, she wasn't blonde, skinny, with big breasts? Shocking," Josh said as he took a drink

EVILyn Reigns

and flipped through the book some more. "Wait, I don't think this is for Garnet's. She mentions S & P in here several times, a first initial, last initial, and a dollar amount next to it. There is also a star next to a few names that references repeat clients and a strike out through some that is referenced as never repeat. I think she solicited at S & P."

Kat sat up, cobwebs quickly clearing from her mind. "No way. She couldn't have. I mean, I know that we used the male prostitutes there, but I could never even imagine she would be able to do that. She had a kink, she needed to be..."

"I know Kat," Josh interrupted. "But it's plain as day right here. Now thinking about it, she always seemed to be able to afford more than her wages. Her apartment. Her clothing. Hell, she even had an account at S & P. It wasn't always you signing in. What if she was a prostitute there?"

Kat shook her head and took the book back from Josh, rereading some of the pages. "I guess it's something we never knew about her. It just doesn't seem like something that she would do. Jenna had a kink and always made us promise to never leave her alone. Why would she do this for money and not tell us? I would have been there to help her. I would have supported her. She didn't need to…"

Kat covered her face with her hands and sobbed. She felt Josh pull her hands away and turned her toward him on the couch.

"I just thought of something, Kat. What if her murderer was one of her clients and he tried to be her dominant? What if something went wrong? Kat, her murderer could be in this book. We need to figure this out."

Shutting the book, Kat placed it back in the box and stood up, moving away from her friend. "No, we don't, Josh. Take the book to the police. Take it to S & P and let them deal with it. We're not police officers, we're not investigators. I'm a librarian and you're a…um… Josh. We can't and I won't."

Josh stood up and walked over toward her, turning her body to face him. "Kat. I have an idea. You should go to S & P and apply to be one of their 'solicitors.' You are a client there and I know that they would love for you and your expertise to perform for them. Then you could go through their computers and match the names with the letters in the book. We could find the guy that did this."

"Josh, NO!" Kat yelled, yanking herself away from him. "What you're telling me to do is something I am incapable of doing. I can't have sex. I don't want to be around another man for any reason. And don't give me that argument that you are a man. You're different. I can't believe you would suggest this. You know my past, my trauma and still… I can't believe this. How could you?"

"Kat, I would do it in a heartbeat. You know I would. But I don't think any of her previous clients would ever go left, not for a moment, not ever. It has to be you. We could find her killer…"

"And then what, Josh? What if he decides to kill me too, huh? He might not even be in that book. It could have been a rando from the street like the police suspect. I won't do it."

"Kat, I feel strongly about this. I know that her murderer is in here. And if we go to the police, her murder case would probably just be shut up in a drawer somewhere because she's just another prostitute. And S & P wouldn't investigate it or go to the police either. It's all underground and the bar would get shut down so fast. It has to be you."

Josh grabbed her face in his hands as she shook her head at his suggestion. "Kat, it has to be you. I can hide in the room and protect you if it gets too much for you. We can do this, together. We can find her killer and deal with him in a way the police would never be able to. We can take revenge. Come on Kat, help me avenge Jenna. Let's avenge Jenna together."

Kat sobbed and laid her head on Josh's chest as he wrapped his arms around her in comfort. She slowly nodded against his now damp shirt.

"Okay," she mumbled. "But you have to stay with me the entire time. If I flip out or start to freak out, get me out of there. I don't know if I could survive it. But for Jenna, I'll do it."

"For Jenna." Josh repeated.

EVILyn Reigns

Chapter 9

Kat paced back and forth in her living room as Josh sat on the couch, staring at her. She had never felt so nervous about anything in her life. Surprisingly, it was easy to set up the escort service at S & P since she had been a client for several years. The receptionist was practically salivating as she took down all the information Kat gave her.

"You told them you were a sub, right?" Josh asked as he ran his hand through his blonde hair. The blue tips in his hair had faded over the past couple of months. Kat found it interesting that with so much on the line, she seemed to be focused on the fact her friend hadn't colored his hair in so long.

"I'm not dumb, Josh. Yes, I told them that I'm a sub and I check marked all of Jenna's quirks," Kat replied with a sneer.

"Easy, babe. No need to snap. I'm nervous too. This could be Jenna's killer right now."

Kat shook her head. "I'm sorry. I'm just so nervous. I was up all night last night and my nightmares have been getting worse. I'm not sleeping much. Every time I even think about allowing myself to be cuffed or touched by another man, I get physically ill. I honestly don't think I can do this, Josh. The police think Jenna's killer was a crime of opportunity, that someone probably tried to rob her and went too far."

"The police are wrong!" Josh yelled, making Kat jump. She had never seen him like this before. Her Josh had always been goofy, ready with a joke and a smile. Just like she used to be so strong before Jenna died, and now she was this quivering mess of a whiney brat that couldn't seem to function in her life without her best friend.

"I'm sorry, Kat. I feel so strongly about this. I know you can do this, and I will be hiding in the closet if you need help. You can do this."

A knock at the door had both of them jump in surprise. Josh kissed her cheek and left for the bedroom closet. Kat pulled the lapels of her thin robe together and walked toward the front door, opening it to a man she had never seen before. He was large, standing over six feet, a full foot taller than her. The man's face sported a large bulbous nose and red cheeks that showed his love for alcohol. His large arms crossed over his chest and his beer gut hung over the waist of his pants. She knew from the initials in Jenna's book and his description that he was one of her regulars. Kat felt so horrible for her friend that she stooped this low.

"Are you Kat?" the man bellowed loudly as he stormed inside her apartment, yanking her arm away from the door. Kat jerked her arm away from him as he slammed and locked the front door.

EVILyn Reigns

"I was told that you were submissive," he said as his eyes narrowed on her arm. She was rubbing the redness away from his strong grip.

"I am a submissive in the bedroom. That does not mean you get to man handle me everywhere else. While you are in my home, you will treat me with decorum and respect. I expect nothing less. If that is something you are unable to do, you can leave."

The man sheepishly nodded his head and walked over toward her couch, taking a seat. He brushed his black hair from his face and stared at her as she collected her courage.

"Are you S.T.?" Kat asked as she walked toward the couch.

"I am. That's what is in the system anyway. I like my subs to call me master."

"Again, not out here. We are not in the bedroom yet and until then, this is my show, and I am in charge. Do you have the money?"

S.T. pulled an envelope of cash out of his shirt pocket and tossed it onto the coffee table. He leaned back against the couch. She could feel his eyes stare at her as she fingered the money in the envelope. Kat walked over toward her television stand and placed the envelope in a drawer. She turned around, shocked that he stood so close behind her.

"I suppose you are ready?" Kat asked as she led him toward her bedroom.

"I was told that you have all your own tools. I prefer the ball gag. I don't like my submissive to speak."

Kat rolled her eyes. "Clearly," she said. "I do not do ball gags. If you would have read my resume, you would have known this. Sucks to be you, because I am very vocal, and I don't give refunds."

He curled his lip and pushed her through the doorway she stood in front of. "Well, if I can't gag you one way, then I'll gag you another," he said as he grabbed her arms in his meaty hands.

"Wait, stop. I'm not ready yet," Kat cried out as she wriggled in his grasp. She grunted as he picked her up and threw her onto the bed before he flipped her onto her stomach.

"Stop. Please stop," she cried.

EVILyn Reigns

"Yeah, baby. I like it when you cry," he groaned as he rubbed his pelvis against her buttocks. Kat heard his zipper being released and tears began to fall from her eyes as she felt him tear the panties from her hips. Not again. This couldn't happen again. Never again.

She cried out as flipped her again, pulling her body flush against him, his large member rubbing against her bare mound. He roughly grabbed one of her breasts and she cried out in pain as he twisted her nipple.

"Josh... Please," Kat cried out as she stared up at the client standing over her limp body. She couldn't seem to force her arms or legs to move, and fear swamped her veins as his face changed shape. She was staring into her father's evil face. A silver shine under her pillow caught her attention and she quickly reached for the object that she once hid long ago, slashing upward as hard as she could. Kat's eyes quickly shut as blood sprayed across her body and bedspread. Gurgling filled the air, and she opened her eyes to see her father stumble away, covering the

Little Black Book

large gaping wound in his throat. Kat looked back at her hand, surprised to see the large kitchen knife in her grasp. The vision of her father dissipated, and she stared at S.T.'s pale face as blood pumped from the wound in his neck.

What did she do?

The closet burst open with a splintering sound; wood chips sprayed the bedroom. Kat dropped the knife and covered her face as she backed up to the wall, sliding down to the floor. She rocked back and forth as the dark red blood slowly began to creep toward her.

"What the fuck, Kat!" Josh yelled as he rushed over toward her, kicking the knife away from her.

"What happened? You were supposed to save me from him. You said you would protect me, and I was almost raped. Where the fuck were you?" Kat cried, tears overflowing her eyes and streaming down her bloodied cheeks. She began hitting his chest with her fists as she screamed at him.

EVILyn Reigns

He grabbed both of Kat's wrists and looked at the carnage in the room. "Jesus, Kat. I was fucking locked in the closet. There's apparently a latch and I couldn't get it unlocked. I wasn't going to let him hurt you, but I was trapped. Your fucking closet. I broke the door. Look, Kat. Look at the closet door. Breathe deep, calm yourself and look at the door."

She took a deep breath and stared at the busted door that now hung on its hinges. Wood splinters littered the bloody floor and she brushed a piece of wood from Josh's hair.

"Jesus, Kat. What are we going to do? You just murdered someone," he said as he dropped her wrists and looked around the bedroom.

"It was self-defense. He tried to rape me."

"The cops won't see the same thing. He paid you to have sex. It's definitely murder. We are going to have to get rid of the body and any evidence of him being here."

"Josh, we should call the police."

"Kat, I can't go to jail. Do you know what happens to the gay population in jail? I've heard all the horror stories. I can't do that to my dad. We have no other option but to get rid of the body and all the evidence."

She nodded her head, seeing her friend's point of view. They would definitely do jail time. She looked around again and felt nausea roll through her stomach as she finally took in the scene of her bedroom. Blood began to coagulate on the floor and the copper penny odor overwhelmed her sense of smell. She rushed to the bathroom and began to vomit in the toilet, the sound of her retching causing her to gag even more. Kat felt Josh behind her as she flushed the toilet and stood up to clean her mouth out in the sink. Staring at herself in the mirror, she was surprised at her pale complexion, her red hair limp and dull, her face splattered with blood from the now dead client that lay on her bedroom floor.

Kat locked eyes with Josh who stood behind her and shook her head. "What are we going to do?" she asked before rinsing her mouth with the tepid water that flowed from the faucet.

EVILyn Reigns

"We are going to work together and clean up this mess. You are going to go log on to your account and claim he never arrived. We need to find out what he drove, and we will make this all go away. At least we found out who Jenna's murderer was."

Kat shook her head. "He didn't kill Jenna."

"Why do you say that? He tried to rape you. He probably raped Jenna and then killed her."

Shaking her head, Kat turned around to face her friend. "Jenna was strangled, remember. The murderer used asphyxiation. This one didn't even attempt to put his hands around my neck. He's still out there."

She left Josh behind in the bedroom and walked toward her kitchen to grab the cleaning supplies from under her sink. Kat gathered the bleach and some spare rags and walked back toward her bedroom where she saw Josh pulling the bedspread from her mattress.

"Thank goodness for hardwood and first floor apartments, eh?" he asked with a small smile and threw her blanket over the body.

Little Black Book

"Josh, I can't sleep here. I can't stay here. Where am I supposed to go?"

He stopped his struggle with the blanket and body and walked over toward her, grabbing both of her hands in his. "Kat, you can stay with me. My dad loves you anyway and he would get excited thinking that I had a girl over. Now, let me finish my job and you go log on to your account at S & P and declare him a no show."

Kat nodded and walked out of the bedroom to the living room and pulled her laptop out from her television stand, logging on to her account, noting that the client was a no show. Before she shut her computer down, she noticed another request for her sub services and approved the date, entering her apartment address in the program. Kat shut her computer down and began to look around for a set of keys from S.T. At least she could find his vehicle.

EVILyn Reigns

Chapter 10

Josh rode silently next to Kat as she drove her car toward his home. It was a long night, and they weren't going to get to his home until after 3 a.m. After Kat found the victim's vehicle, she was thankful he drove a large truck and they were able to work together to load the blanket wrapped body into the truck bed. They drove to the San Antonio Quarry, placed the truck in neutral gear, and pushed the vehicle over into the mining operation. They then rode together back to her apartment and began to thoroughly clean. Kat Googled the best way to clean up blood spills and she was surprised by the amount of hydrogen peroxide that she would need. She stopped at the pharmacy on the way and picked up several bottles of the stuff. It took them several hours to mop up the blood from the floor and clean the blood from her mattress before covering the bed with clean sheets.

Kat pulled into the long driveway in front of Josh's large house and put the car in park, resting her head against the seat as she blew a breath out through her nose.

"Tell me everything is going to be okay," she whispered.

"Everything is going to be okay," Josh said as he sighed and laid his own head back against the seat.

"You're lying," Kat said as she lightly pushed his arm.

"Yes, yes I am." Josh opened his door and climbed out of her car. "Come on, let's go take our showers and pass out. We could use a good night's sleep."

Kat opened her door and followed Josh into his house. She was incredibly exhausted and looked forward to sleeping. As she laid down on the bed, a vision of Jenna appeared near the bedroom door. Her friend walked toward her and slowly traced her cheek as Kat closed her eyes, falling asleep with a smile.

"Jenna," she whispered as blackness surrounded her.

•

Sweat covered her face as Kat sat up straight following a short night of interrupted sleep. Her dreams, nightmares, were haunting her every evening and she wasn't sure how much longer she could go without her outlet. Her and Jenna used to help each other every time Kat's demons grew too large. But without her friend, her partner, Kat felt that she was going to go crazy.

She brushed the damp red hair from her eyes and stretched her body as she stood from the bed. She was surprised with how comfortable the mattress was. Well, she shouldn't be too surprised. Josh always needed to have the best of everything, even if it was something that he never used. Kat put her arms through the sleeves of her robe and decided to leave her room to explore the monstrosity that Josh resided in.

Opening doors in the hallway had her eyebrows raised at the opulence of the bedrooms and bathrooms. The last time she stayed the night at Josh's home, it didn't look anything like this. One bathroom had gold faucets. Gold! She was afraid to breathe and possibly leave behind the residue of her life force, ruining the newly decorated home.

Kat opened one door before she realized that there were people in the room, groaning. She stood in the doorway and stared as Josh and another man were together in the large bed. She tilted her head and watched as the two men made love to each other, seemingly desperate to keep their moans to a minimum.

Little Black Book

"If I would have known that we were allowed to bring dates, I would have invited someone to share my bed," Kat said, interrupting the lovers.

Josh squealed and jumped from the bed as the other man smirked at Kat. He lay completely nude in bed, his hands behind his head. She stared at the thick, erect, member resting against his belly button.

"I could go both ways, darlin,' if you were interested in joining the party," the other man said as Josh quickly covered himself with his robe.

"Shut up, Scott. She's more likely to kill you before fucking you," Josh said as he walked toward the door.

"That wasn't very nice, Josh. I told you it was an accident," Kat said. "So, this is the infamous Scott. Sadly, I thought there would be something more to him according to what you told me, but I find him sorely lacking in different departments."

"Shush, Kat," Josh replied, as he pulled her out of the room, shutting the door behind him.

EVILyn Reigns

"So, this is what you have been hiding from me. Is he the same guy that you have been seeing at the club as well?"

"Yes, okay? But keep your voice down. My dad is home, and I don't want to wake him up."

"He's kinda cute for a boy toy. I'll leave you to play 'hide the sausage.' I'll play interference with your dad if I see him." Kat turned to walk back to her room to get dressed.

"Hey Kat?" Josh asked and she turned to face him. "I know Scott is into women too, if you need a good release."

Kat smiled sadly and shook her head. "No, it's okay. You're probably right. I would end up killing him."

•

Sitting at the dining room table, Kat took another sip of tea as she disregarded the older man sitting across from her. They quietly refused to lock eyes as she looked down into her teacup, transfixed by the dark liquid that was too strong for her to drink.

Little Black Book

She finally sighed and scooted her chair back from the table so she could go back to the room she was staying in.

"Kat, wait," he said as he lowered his tea glass. "I just wanted to thank you for being there for my son."

She shrugged her shoulders. "He's my best friend."

"You cover for him a lot. You and Jenna both did. Now, just you. But I know everything, and I just wanted to thank you and tell you that you don't have to cover for him anymore. That I know."

She shook her head. "I don't understand, sir."

He sighed, stood up from the table and walked over to where she sat. She knew that Josh inherited his father's short stature and looks, but recently, her friend had been looking even more so like his father. Her thoughts were interrupted when he began talking again.

"I know my son is gay. I've known for a while. He thinks he's so sly and sneaky but I've known since he was a young man that he was homosexual. Unfortunately, I did not take the news very well when he was younger and I threatened to cut off his luxury lifestyle if he continued down the road he was traveling. I fear that my ultimatum also ruined the closeness we used to have. He doesn't talk to me anymore like he used to. I don't know how to get that back."

Kat rubbed her neck, uncomfortable in how the conversation was progressing. She told Josh that she would cover for him, not be the family therapist in their little domestic drama.

"Look, sir," she began.

"Joshua," her friend's dad interrupted. "I feel you've been around long enough over the years that you can be a little informal, especially since I'm asking for your advice regarding my son."

Kat did not feel comfortable enough to be that familiar with her friend's stuffy dad. "Sir, if you want to fix things with your son, you need to talk to him. He still thinks that you hate him. I suggest you wait until he comes down to the kitchen because you might get a sight that you can't erase if you search him out now. I had to scrub my eyeballs with bleach already this morning when I made that mistake. I'm going to go back to my room and rest."

Kat began to walk out of the dining room but turned back. "Sir, one more thing. I appreciate you letting me stay here because of my apartment getting fumigated," she started, remembering her and Josh's cover story, "But I would have that talk sooner rather than later. I had so much that I wanted to say to Jenna before she died. I wanted to tell her how much she meant to me, how much I loved her. But now she's dead and I only have her grave to talk to. Unfortunately, the cement does not talk back."

She watched as her friend's father nodded his head before she left for the bedroom. Kat walked into her room and pulled a backpack out of the closet. She packed two extra set of clothes before she changed into her favorite leather vest and blue jeans. Kat's appointment was in just a couple of hours, and she hoped to sneak out of the house and take care of business before she could sneak back in. Deciding a little while ago that she couldn't depend on Josh, Kat decided to not bring him to her next meeting with a potential killer. If things went wrong again, she didn't want him to be involved. He had a family, a life that she didn't want ruined because of her personal demons. Kat looked up and smiled sadly as a hazy Jenna stood next to her. She shook her head and left her vision behind.

    She walked out of the bedroom and kept her eyes out for anyone that would stop her from leaving. She boldly walked out of the front door. It was time for revenge.

Chapter 11

The front door vibrated with the force of the knocking, the loud bam-bam-bam echoing around the living room of Kat's apartment. She slowly walked toward the front door, smoothing her hair back from her face and taking a deep breath. She couldn't rely on Josh to help her this time and Kat knew she only had herself to depend on if she got herself into trouble again.

The knocking stopped and then restarted, even more forceful than a moment ago. Kat

EVILyn Reigns

smoothed her robe and slowly opened the door to the stranger standing in her entry way. His crooked nose took over the majority of his face and his beady brown eyes seemed to look straight through her. The dark black hair that barely covered his head was receding, showing a large area of his forehead. He pushed himself into her apartment, slamming the door shut behind him.

"I only paid for an hour so let's get this show on the road," he bellowed, his fists on his wide hips.

Kat shook her head and walked back toward the kitchen. "I need to verify your identity and check your payment first. What is your name?" she asked as she retrieved a bottle of water from the refrigerator. She untwisted the cap and handed the drink to her guest.

"I'm Jeremy. Jeremy Smith," he said as he took the bottle of water, guzzling it until it was near empty before setting the bottle on the kitchen table. She watched him take an envelope out of the back pocket of his jeans, tossing it onto the table. He crossed his arms and waited as Kat picked up the envelope and flipped through the cash. She watched through the corner of her eye as he shook his head, as if he was trying to clear cobwebs from his mind. He shook his head a second time and wavered in place before he completely crashed onto the marble floor, passed out. Kat smiled and walked back to the sink, retrieving the yellow rubber gloves, and sliding them onto her hands.

"Most excellent," Kat said as she walked toward the unconscious man on the floor. It was time for her to get to work.

•

Kat bent down and slapped Jeremiah's face as hard as she could. His head snapped to the side, and he blinked his brown eyes open, confused as he stared around the room. She straightened up to her full height, and smiled as she watched him struggle against the bonds that tethered him to the kitchen chair. Kat slowly walked back toward the chair across from her bound prisoner and sat down to wait while he tried to work himself free. She knew it was a fruitless effort. Her father taught her all about being bound and he was going to wear himself out with the struggles.

"What is going on? What are you going to do with me?" Jeremiah asked as soon as he gave up his effort.

"I'm so glad that you asked, J.S. I can call you J.S., right?" Kat picked up the black book and flipped to the book-marked page. She began to read out loud.

"*J.S. finally left my home. I hope to never have to service him again. The pain he afflicted on me was one of the worst I have ever experienced. The degradation he made me feel as I had to clean my own blood from his body after he cut me with his knife was not something I want to ever have again. I wish I would have called my Kat to help me. I don't know why I am this way, but I am worried about making my friend help me with my addiction.*

"*I sometimes think about seeking help for my issues, my need for pain. If I do so, I will never have to deal with men like J.S. again. I counted the money, and he shorted me by five-hundred dollars as well. I am placing a strike through his name and telling the club that he needs to be removed. I would hate to find out that he hurt another girl the way he hurt me. Oh God, the pain. I can't sit down; I can't stand up. I don't know who to call."*

Kat closed the book. "This is you, isn't it? Tell me, did the club kick you out over this, or did you give more money to keep your membership? How many more girls did you hurt?"

Jeremiah began to shake his head. "You don't understand; she asked me to hurt her."

Kat stood up and ran over to where he was bound, the plastic tarp under her feet crinkling with every step. She slapped him across the face. "Shut up!" she screamed. She slowly walked back to her chair and sat back down, crossing her legs, and showcased them in the near see-through robe she wore.

"Let's try this again. How many more girls did you hurt?"

EVILyn Reigns

Jeremiah sniffled, mucous running down his nose, blood dripping from a cut on his bottom lip. "I only used Jenna. She begged for it. She demanded I hurt her. It wasn't my fault. Not my fault." He began to struggle in his bonds again as Kat stood up from her seat. She reached over and picked up a knife from the table behind her and walked back over to the struggling man.

"My Jenna didn't give me any details on what you did to her. I know if I ask you, you will probably lie about it because that's what chicken shit pussies do. They lie. But I have a very big imagination and I will be using it today." Kat began to slowly slice her knife through his shirt, exposing his bare chest. She twisted her lips at his saggy chest and large pot belly. "Hmm, J.S., not much to write home about. I expected more from you to be honest."

She completely cut the shirt away from his skin, smiling as she accidentally sliced his flesh with her knife. He screamed from the pain as blood bubbled up from the cut on his pale skin. Kat shushed him and took a piece of the shirt she cut away and stuffed it into his mouth.

"Shh, we don't want to invite the neighbors to our party now, do we?" Kat finished bestowing 'J' shaped slices into his skin before walking back to the kitchen and placing her bloody knife into the sink. She removed the yellow rubber gloves before she placed oven mitts onto her dominant hand. She opened the oven and removed the hot wire hanger that she placed there hours before. The wire hanger was in the shape of the letter J.

Kat walked back toward her victim. He seemed to be passed out in his chair. Picking up her glass of water, she took a drink before throwing the rest of it into his face, promptly waking him from his unconscious state. Jeremiah quickly lifted his head and shook water droplets from his face.

"Now, this might hurt a little more than you might be used to, but since you're now my bitch, I have the right to do what I want with your flabby little body. Since Jenna can't be here to witness this restitution that she deserves, I will have to do her justice. Hmm, J for Justice for Jenna. Seems fitting, doesn't it?"

Kat lifted the steaming hanger toward him and smiled as he began to cry, sobs escaping his chest, muffled by the ripped shirt that was stuffed into his mouth. She pressed the heated hanger against his skin, hard. Closing her eyes as she relished the sound of his muffled screams, Kat began to feel the beginnings of an ache between her legs. The pain she was afflicting on her victim was giving her the most precise, perfect pleasure. She moaned as desire began to roll through her lower belly and removed the hanger from his sizzling skin.

"Hmm, it seemed to have cooled off, J.S. Don't worry, I have more," Kat said, whistling a tune as she walked through the kitchen. "I have enough for the entire night," she whispered as she opened the oven.

•

Kat sat on the bed in her bedroom contemplating the information that she just learned from her latest victim. Her quest was slowly coming to a close. It took a little extra persuasion before Jeremiah began to speak about the other members of the club that Jenna sold her services to. One in particular has a brutal taste for blood and pain. Kat looked through the journal and found the initials that matched the description Jeremiah gave her. She shuddered as she remembered his tears and his cries of pain. What a whiny baby he was. She suffered so much more herself without a single sound escaping and he couldn't handle a little torture, a fraction of what she herself went through as a child.

  She looked up at a sad Jenna. Kat didn't know if she was going crazy or if her friend was haunting her, demanding restitution for her rape and murder. She watched Jenna shake her head before she left Kat alone in the bedroom.

  Lifting her head, Kat walked out of her room and into the living room when she heard her front door open, and Josh call out for her. She hadn't quite cleaned up her mess and didn't want to scare her friend. Honestly, he probably needed a little scaring. This whole adventure was his idea, anyway.

"Kat, what the fuck!" she heard him yell from the other room. Shaking her head, Kat walked into the living room where Josh stood over a dead body, in shock from her artwork. She had successfully burned Jenna's name into his skin and spilled enough blood to pacify her inner demons that screamed for pain, screamed for vengeance. Josh placed her on this path with his grandiose ideas. He could help clean up the mess she made.

"I didn't make that much of a mess this time, Josh. I just need help rolling the body up in the tarp and into the backseat of my car so we can take him to the quarry."

"Did he kill Jenna?"

"No, but he did hurt her though. Before he died, he gave me some interesting names of men who would have explored the kinks that took Jenna's life." Kat pushed the limp body from the chair and onto the tarp that covered the floor. "Are you going to stand there and stare or are you going to help me with your project?"

She waited as Josh took a deep breath before walking over to her. He helped roll the tarp and picked up one end as she picked up the other and they worked together, moving the rolled corpse out of the apartment and into her car that was parked out front.

"Kat, I think that maybe we should dial back a little with your investigation. I know that the first time was a mistake, that you didn't mean to kill him. I tried to get out of the closet to help you, and that it was self-defense, but this is taking it too far. You purposefully murdered this man. I had a long talk with my father, and he told me that he knew that I was gay, and he didn't want to lose me or ruin our relationship. I just don't want anything to ruin the budding bond that we are forming, especially if he finds out about this. Please tell me this is the last one."

After heaving the corpse into the back seat of her sedan, Kat turned back toward her friend. "Look, Josh, you set me on this path. I didn't want to do this, but now the action cannot be erased or taken back. I need to finish this, and you have to help me. I do have a lead, and this time I am going to his home. I will need you to meet me there so we can do this together. We're in this together. Just remember that." Kat gave him her sternest evil eye before walking to the driver's side door and climbing into her car. She rolled down the passenger window.

"You coming?"

Kat watched Josh take a deep sigh before he climbed into the car. "That's a good boy. Now let's finish what you started."

Chapter 12

Reading through the journal, Kat discovered some other secrets that she didn't know about her closest friend. Jenna led a pretty secretive life, one that Kat wasn't a part of, and her heart broke a little with the discovery. She also found out why Jenna needed the pain so badly.

Jenna's parents never gave her any kind of physical or vocal affection, leaving her alone as a small child for hours at a time. During Jenna's teenage years, she had turned to cutting herself to combat the feelings of abandonment. Cutting soon turned erotic for her and she discovered her need for pain in order to fulfill her sexual completion.

Kat was grateful that she was there for her friend during the severe needs of her sexuality, but she wished that Jenna would have come to her with this knowledge sooner. Her friend wrote about being alone in her feelings, but she wasn't alone. Kat had the very same feelings of inadequacy but instead of the need to feel pain, she needed to give it. She also had plenty of money from her family's estate. If Jenna had been that hard up for cash, Kat would have given it to her friend, no questions asked.

Closing the book, Kat placed the journal in her bag and finished getting ready for her newest visitor. For her last two clients she clicked the 'no show' button on the app that she used to mark when her Johns arrived and departed. Kat figured that she didn't have much more time left before they locked her out of the computer completely. It can't be a coincidence that so many men were 'no call no shows' and they also conveniently disappeared before their appointment time.

This was a special John and he wanted to meet her at a hotel room instead of her apartment or his personal home. Because she refused to use the facilities at S & P, the list of possible suspects of men that hurt Jenna lowered considerably, something she was grateful for. It meant that it lowered the amount of time spent with the scum of the earth. She was beginning to feel disgusted, dirty from touching these men, and Kat looked forward to the relief of finding her friend's killer. This guy she was getting ready to meet gave her a funny feeling. This might be the one she and Josh were looking for.

Zipping up her duffle bag, Kat begin to mentally go through her checklist of her supplies. She had a few new gifts that she looked forward to incorrectly using on someone. As she lifted her bag and turned toward her door, she was surprised to see Josh blocking her exit.

"Kat, I think we should stop. I was definitely heated when I pushed you into this, but you've already killed innocent people. They didn't deserve to die the way they did. Please, Kat."

She shook her head. "No, Josh. You were right, Jenna deserves to be avenged. And those two men were not innocent. They hurt Jenna. The first John tried to rape me! You were there, you were going to just watch him rape me…"

"He thought you were a prostitute Kat!"

"That's no fucking excuse, Josh!" she screamed. "Jenna was supposedly a prostitute. Did she deserve to be raped and killed?"

Josh rubbed the back of his neck. "That's not what I meant. I'm sorry Kat. But the fact of the matter is that we don't know who killed Jenna. We may never know who killed Jenna. All I know is that my life is finally coming together. I finally have a great boyfriend. My dad accepts my sexuality, and I don't want it all being ruined because of your need for vengeance and my hairbrained idea that was the result of my hot head and a bottle of wine. Please Kat. Please?"

Little Black Book

She shook her head. "I'm in too deep. I can't sleep. I can't think. I feel as if her spirit is following me, demanding revenge and I need to find her killer. I am in too deep. If you want to escape, go. Your hands are clean, but my soul is forever damaged, and I will never feel clean again. I have to see this through to the end."

She watched her friend nod his head before he walked out of the door. Kat suddenly felt so alone. She left the room, walking through a hazy vision of Jenna.

•

Sitting on the hotel bed, Kat slowly brushed her long hair before tying it back into a low braid. The seconds were ticking by slowly, the silent tick tock burrowing holes into her brain. She nervously waited for the John that she suspected of hurting her best friend. The crunch of footsteps outside her room had her placing the brush on the bedside table before she stood up to face her newest client.

EVILyn Reigns

A light knock on the hotel room door interrupted her thoughts and she walked to it, running her hand down the side of her leg with a sweaty palm. As she passed by the long wall mirror, Kat looked at her reflection and shook her head. Her "John" had told her that she needed to wear a black leather negligee and a black leather collar with a silver ring. Truthfully, she never looked so sexy as she did in that moment. The scars on her cheek did nothing to take away from her body encased in the leather. Kat's breasts were pushed high under her outfit, her curves pronounced by the way the outfit crisscrossed her body.

A slow knock woke her from her moment, and she opened the door, shocked at the figure standing in front of her.

"Joshua?" she asked with confusion. Her friend's father stood in front of her as she held the door open. Kat watched as his eyes widened with surprise before he walked into the hotel room. He gently removed her hand from the door and closed it silently, the quiet snick of the lock as loud as a bomb.

"Kat, my, my. I didn't know you were working with S & P. If I knew that you had side work, I would have requested you ages ago."

"Sir, I don't understand."

"I will forgive you for the first two transgressions. While you are in my care I am not Joshua Sr. nor am I 'Sir.' You may call me Master."

Kat shook her head and began to back away from the stranger standing in front of her. She'd known him for years, as long as she'd known his son. But today someone that she had never met stood in front of her demanding submissiveness. Confusion overwhelmed her as the room began to spin. She could feel soft fingers stroking her cheek as visions of her father colored the sight before her. Kat felt herself shudder as he stroked the scars on her cheek.

"You are a good girl, aren't you? I knew that this was going to be an amazing session, but I didn't know how amazing it would be until know. You, my dear, are exquisite."

Kat shook her head again and backed away from his soft touch. She turned to get her duffle bag so she could leave. A sharp tug on her braid stopped her as he pulled her back, flush against his body. He began to rub his heavy erection against her back, groaning as tears slowly seeped from her eyes.

"Sir, please. You're Josh's father. I can't do this. I need to leave. Please, let me leave. If I would have known it was you, I wouldn't have accepted the job."

She heard him growl into her ear. "Please tell me you're not a sniveling little brat like his other little friend was. She cried when she discovered my need of certain proclivities. I drank her tears as I took her skin, and I shall do the same to you. I will make you orgasm with my need for your flesh. I only hope that you will last longer than that sniveling little brat."

Red colored Kat's vision as she froze with his admission. This whole time, it was her own friend's father that took Jenna's life. Did Josh know? Is that why he asked her to lay off her revenge? He probably found out and was willing to risk her friendship, willing to risk Jenna's killer getting away, just so that he could have the daddy he always wanted.

Kat then knew what she needed to do.

"Yes, Master. I will truly enjoy the pain and suffering. I just need to retrieve one thing from my bag, please. Master, please?" she said with as much meekness in her voice as she could muster.

"Well, my dear. I do enjoy gifts. Yes, you may and when you return I want you to crawl on your knees and unzip my pants so I can fuck your face. And I want you to moan like a good little girl."

Kat nodded with a smile and slowly walked over to her duffle bag. She unzipped it and pulled out a small item that she concealed behind her back. She turned and kneeled down onto her knees before she crawled over to her friend's father. She waited on her heels as he unbuttoned his pants and removed his hard, thick cock.

Kat looked up into his face, not surprised when he licked his lips, and watched his face contort when she applied the taser to his testicles. She reveled in his screams as she held the device against his sensitive skin. Her skin became heated, and she could feal the arousal coursing through her body as he collapsed to the floor, convulsing with pain. When he finally blacked out, Kat removed the taser and stood up, walking over to her bag, and stowing the device. She pulled duct tape and zip ties from her bag and walked toward her victim. It was time for a little fun.

●

"Wakey, wakey, princess," Kat said as she slapped Joshua Sr. across his face. She smiled as his blood shot eyes blinked open, and his nose leaked a little blood from the force of the electrical current that coursed through his veins.

"It's time for us to have a little fun." She smiled when his eyes teared up and he began to struggle in his bonds.

"Oh, look. Who's the sniveling little girl now? You can call me Master and I will feel the flesh peel back from your skin. I am going to bathe in your blood and dance on your dead body. Because by the

Little Black Book

end of our little game, you will be dead, and Jenna will be avenged."

Kat looked up to the corner of the office room they were in and saw her friend, hazy and sad. Jenna shook her head and Kat swore she saw a small smile creep across her silent friend's face. She turned back to her newest victim bound to the chair.

She watched him look around the room and smiled when his eyes widened. "Oh, do you recognize where we are? Yes, I was able to load you up into your snazzy car and bring you back to your mansion of a home. We don't need the hotel staff calling the police because of your girlish screams. Now, before I begin, let's have a little reading lesson, shall we?"

Kat opened Jenna's black book. She began to carry it with her everywhere and looked into it anytime she needed some inspiration, some sign to tell her that she was doing the right thing.

She cleared her throat and began to read from the last part of the book, the very last chapter of her friend's journal.

EVILyn Reigns

"Ahem. '*I am really nervous for my newest John. I am not allowed to enclose his name, so I will use the initials J.S.*' It's interesting to me, J.S., that she had a lot of customers with the initial J attached to them... well the customers that hurt her. Excuse me, let me go on. '*I have only seen him once before and I promised that I would never accept another job from him again. The money was too good to pass up and he demanded that I be the one to service him. I do not want to lose my contract with S & P so I decided one more time wouldn't be so bad. Maybe, if I cooperated with his games, he wouldn't be so hard on me. I am a little scared though. I hope I don't bleed so much this time.*'"

Kat shut the book with a loud thud, and she smiled when her John jumped. He began to wrestle his bindings and scream behind the duct tape that covered his lips.

"I decided that I needed to do to you exactly what you did to my Jenna. Unfortunately, I do not want to hear your disgusting voice, so I decided to create my own images of your torture." She walked back toward her bag by the door and reached in, pulling out a small paring knife.

"Let's begin with a little bloodletting shall we?" Kat smiled as she made the first slice into his skin. Joshua screamed and began to wriggle in order to get away from her knife.

"Now, now, wriggling will only make it hurt more, don't you know? Be a good little girl and get still."

She sliced up his bare arm and finally removed a strip of skin of about four inches in length. "Look at this! It's bigger than your cock! I am so talented. Let's see if I can get a bigger one."

Kat reached to his face and laughed when he jerked his head away from her knife bearing hand. "Oh, sweetie, I was only trying to help you dry your tears. But get still. I don't want to accidentally cut you while I remove your clothes."

Kat began to tear strips of his shirt from his body, throwing them onto the floor behind her. "Oh my, look at all that pearly white skin. It's a little flabby. I sure hope that we can get some good skin."

EVILyn Reigns

Kat began to slowly slice the paring knife across the torso, despite his muffled screams and his constant moving under his bindings. Every strip of skin she peeled she held up in front of his face so he could see her pieces of hard work. Blood ran down his body and pooled onto the carpeted floor underneath his chair.

"You know, usually I worry about leaving a mess behind. But since we are in your house, I am not too worried about cleaning. Tell me, before I retrieve my newest toy, did Josh know about your little hobby?"

She waited as he limply shook his head, his head barely moving.

Kat moved closer to his face and wiped a tear from his bloodied cheek. "I don't believe you," she whispered.

She smiled as he screamed.

•

Kat opened the door to the bedroom she had been held up in for the last few hours. She was tired and she needed a shower, badly. She took a deep breath and leaned her back up against the door, relief coursing through her body at finally avenging her Jenna. The weight lifted from her heart was miraculous. She had heard that revenge doesn't bring the dead back, but it did give Kat a feeling of freedom, the need for retaliation finally put to rest.

Footsteps hurried down the hallway and Kat looked up sharply as Josh came into view. She saw his eyes widen with surprise at her presence and she knew the blood covering her body might have been a bit of a shock.

"Kat, what did you do?" he asked.

"It's over, Josh. I finally avenged Jenna, just like you wanted."

"Kat... please tell me you didn't..."

"Oh, yes I did. Tell me. Did you know? Did you know what your own father did to our friend?" She watched him carefully as he nodded slightly, refusing to make eye contact with her. Kat took a deep breath and shook her head, tears springing to her eyes with her friend's admission.

"Oh, Josh. Why didn't you say anything? You put me on this path of vengeance. Why didn't you tell me when you found out?"

"Because he was my father. I was finally forming a relationship with him. I lost my best friend, I was losing you, I didn't want to lose my father too."

Kat looked up to the ceiling, asking the white paint that filled her vision for strength for what she needed to say to her only living friend.

"Well, I finished what you started. Jenna has been avenged. Tell me, how did you find out your father killed Jenna? I found out the hard way. Did you and dear old daddy have a talk about his sexual appetites? Did you walk in on him with another woman? You know what? Never mind. I don't think I want to know. Just know that he can never hurt another woman ever again," Kat said as she crossed her arms over her chest. She watched as Josh began to breathe heavily, shock coloring his face red. He pushed her aside and ran into the room she just exited.

Little Black Book

Kat smiled when she heard the screams of anguish that filled the quiet home. She leaned down to pick up the duffle bag and walked toward the front door. She knew that she was now forever alone, but Kat had a whole black book of men waiting for her. She still had more work to do.

"Kat!" Josh yelled from behind her, and she turned to face him. He held a gun clasped in shaking hands, tears running down his face. "You ruined everything! Why didn't you just let it go? I told you to let it go and you had to keep pushing."

She dropped her duffle bag onto the floor and slowly raised her hands to the air. "Are you going to shoot me now, Josh? I did what you were too weak to do. I avenged Jenna. Me. I did that, and you were a sniveling little weasel that only cared about your relationship with your daddy. A relationship that wouldn't have lasted. Trust me, I know how fathers betray their children. They like to hurt their children and there is no happily ever after. Jenna was forever and you couldn't grow the balls to avenge her when you discovered your precious daddy was involved.

EVILyn Reigns

He wasn't stopping with Jenna, remember? He called me. He probably would have raped and killed me too. Would you have wanted revenge then, or would you still be the crying little boy begging for his daddy's love and acceptance? Huh?"

"Shut up!" Josh screamed. "I called the police. I told them everything, where to find the bodies, what you did. I told them all about S & P and their prostitution ring. They are probably on their way now. We will probably both go to jail, but you… you will get the death penalty."

Kat began to walk slowly toward Josh as she hummed soothing murmurs. "Shh, it's all going to be okay. You're right. The police did need to be called and I can understand why you did what you did. I don't agree but I understand. It's all going to be okay."

She stood in front of Josh, slowly tracing the tears that stained his cheeks. He lowered the gun to the side of his body and threw one arm around her, crying into her shoulder. Kat looked behind him and saw a hazy Jenna sadly watching them. She reached one hand down and slowly placed it over his that held the gun. Kat removed the gun from his hand and leaned away from him, removed his arm from her body and pressed the gun against the side of his head. She pulled the trigger, wincing with the blast and splatter of blood and brain matter that blew into her face.

"We will all be together soon, Josh. It will all be okay, I promise."

EVILyn Reigns

CHAPTER 13

The police surrounded the large house that Kat barricaded herself in. Lights from the sirens left colorful shadows that gave the living room a haunting essence. She looked over at Josh, his cold body on the floor, blood and brain matter spilling from the gunshot wound that exposed white shattered bone. The still hot gun sat in her lap, the barrel burning her bare legs. Muffled voices burst through bullhorns, but Kat couldn't hear, couldn't see anything around her. A single tear rolled down her face as the splintering sounds of a battering ram hitting the door gave Kat the incentive for the very last thing she knew she needed to do. Lifting the gun to her chin, Kat took one more deep breath as she looked over toward the corner of the living room. Her eyes widened as she saw a sharp vision of Jenna standing in front of her, the most beautiful sight she had ever seen since the tragic death of her best friend.

Footsteps pounded on the floor as her finger tightened on the trigger. Jenna squatted down to her level and reached out to touch Kat; a coldness pressed the old scars on her face where Jenna lightly stroked.

"*I can't wait to hold you in my arms again,*" Jenna said with a smile, her ghostly hand tight against Kat's clammy one as they both held the gun tightly against her chin.

The End